The Short Stories Of Jerome K Jerome

The short story is often viewed as an inferior relation to the Novel. But it is an art in itself. To take a story and distil its essence into fewer pages while keeping character and plot rounded and driven is not an easy task. Many try and many fail.

In this series we look at short stories from many of our most accomplished writers. Miniature masterpieces with a lot to say. In this volume we examine some of the short stories of Jerome K Jerome.

An early life of poverty exacerbated by the death of his parents in his early teens helped to cruelly mold the young Jerome. After early stints on the railways, as an actor, a journalist, a school teacher, a writer and a solicitors clerk he had some minor success with a collection of comic memoirs "On The Stage – And Off" about his earlier stint as an actor.

Shortly thereafter he married and his honeymoon on the Thames became the inspiration for Three Men In A Boat. This of course was a wild success both critically and commercially and also his creative highpoint. Although he was now able to write full time he was never able to attain all the heights of that classic humorous novel. However he was prolific at the shorter form and it is from that rich seam that these stories have been mined.

All of these stories are also available as an audiobook from our sister company Word Of Mouth. Many samples are at our youtube channel http://www.youtube.com/user/PortablePoetry?feature=mhee The full volume can be purchased from iTunes, Amazon and other digital stores. They are read for you by Richard Mitchley & Ghizela Rowe

Index Of Stories

The Absent-Minded Man

You ask him to dine with you on Thursday to meet a few people who are anxious to know him.

"Now don't make a muddle of it," you say, recollectful of former mishaps, "and come on the Wednesday."

He laughs good-naturedly as he hunts through the room for his diary.

"Shan't be able to come Wednesday," he says, "shall be at the Mansion House, sketching dresses, and on Friday I start for Scotland, so as to be at the opening of the Exhibition on Saturday. It's bound to be all right this time. Where the deuce is that diary! Never mind, I'll make a note of it on this--you can see me do it."

You stand over him while he writes the appointment down on a sheet of foolscap, and watch him pin it up over his desk. Then you come away contented.

"I do hope he'll turn up," you say to your wife on the Thursday evening, while dressing.

"Are you sure you made it clear to him?" she replies, suspiciously, and you instinctively feel that whatever happens she is going to blame you for it.

Eight o'clock arrives, and with it the other guests. At half-past eight your wife is beckoned mysteriously out of the room, where the parlour- maid informs her that the cook has expressed a determination, in case of further delay, to wash her hands, figuratively speaking, of the whole affair.

Your wife, returning, suggests that if the dinner is to be eaten at all it had better be begun. She evidently considers that in pretending to expect him you have been merely playing a part, and that it would have been manlier and more straightforward for you to have admitted at the beginning that you had forgotten to invite him.

During the soup and the fish you recount anecdotes of his unpunctuality. By the time the entree arrives the empty chair has begun to cast a gloom over the dinner, and with the joint the conversation drifts into talk about dead relatives.

On Friday, at a quarter past eight, he dashes to the door and rings violently. Hearing his voice in the hall, you go to meet him.

"Sorry I'm late," he sings out cheerily. "Fool of a cabman took me to Alfred Place instead of -"

"Well, what do you want now you are come?" you interrupt, feeling anything but genially inclined towards him. He is an old friend, so you can be rude to him.

He laughs, and slaps you on the shoulder.

"Why, my dinner, my dear boy, I'm starving."

"Oh," you grunt in reply. "Well, you go and get it somewhere else, then. You're not going to have it here."

"What the devil do you mean?" he says. "You asked me to dinner."

"I did nothing of the kind," you tell him. "I asked you to dinner on Thursday, not on Friday."

He stares at you incredulously.

"How did I get Friday fixed in my mind?" inquiringly.

"Because yours is the sort of mind that would get Friday firmly fixed into it, when Thursday was the day," you explain. "I thought you had to be off to Edinburgh to-night," you add.

"Great Scott!" he cries, "so I have."

And without another word he dashes out, and you hear him rushing down the road, shouting for the cab he has just dismissed.

As you return to your study you reflect that he will have to travel all the way to Scotland in evening dress, and will have to send out the hotel porter in the morning to buy him a suit of ready-made clothes, and are glad.

Matters work out still more awkwardly when it is he who is the host. I remember being with him on his house-boat one day. It was a little after twelve, and we were sitting on the edge of the boat, dangling our feet in the river--the spot was a lonely one, half-way between Wallingford and Day's Lock. Suddenly round the bend appeared two skiffs, each one containing six elaborately-dressed persons. As soon as they caught sight of us they began waving handkerchiefs and parasols.

"Hullo!" I said, "here's some people hailing you."

"Oh, they all do that about here," he answered, without looking up. "Some beanfeast from Abingdon, I expect."

The boats draw nearer. When about two hundred yards off an elderly gentleman raised himself up in the prow of the leading one and shouted to us.

McQuae heard his voice, and gave a start that all but pitched him into the water.

"Good God!" he cried, "I'd forgotten all about it."

"About what?" I asked.

"Why, it's the Palmers and the Grahams and the Hendersons. I've asked them all over to lunch, and there's not a blessed thing on board but two mutton chops and a pound of potatoes, and I've given the boy a holiday."

Another day I was lunching with him at the Junior Hogarth, when a man named Hallyard, a mutual friend, strolled across to us.

"What are you fellows going to do this afternoon?" he asked, seating himself the opposite side of the table.

"I'm going to stop here and write letters," I answered.

"Come with me if you want something to do," said McQuae. "I'm going to drive Leena down to Richmond." ("Leena" was the young lady he recollected being engaged to. It transpired afterwards that he was engaged to three girls at the time. The other two he had forgotten all about.) "It's a roomy seat at the back."

"Oh, all right," said Hallyard, and they went away together in a hansom.

An hour and a half later Hallyard walked into the smoking-room looking depressed and worn, and flung himself into a chair.

"I thought you were going to Richmond with McQuae," I said.

"So did I," he answered.

"Had an accident?" I asked.

"Yes."

He was decidedly curt in his replies.

"Cart upset?" I continued.

"No, only me."

His grammar and his nerves seemed thoroughly shaken.

I waited for an explanation, and after a while he gave it.

"We got to Putney," he said, "with just an occasional run into a tram- car, and were going up the hill, when suddenly he turned a corner. You know his style at a corner; over the curb, across the road, and into the opposite lamp-post. Of course, as a rule one is prepared for it, but I never reckoned on his turning up there, and the first thing I recollect is finding myself sitting in the middle of the street with a dozen fools grinning at me.

"It takes a man a few minutes in such a case to think where he is and what has happened, and when I got up they were some distance away. I ran after them for a quarter of a mile, shouting at the top of my voice, and accompanied by a mob of boys, all yelling like hell on a Bank Holiday. But one might as well have tried to hail the dead, so I took the 'bus back.

"They might have guessed what had happened," he added, "by the shifting of the cart, if they'd had any sense. I'm not a light-weight."

He complained of soreness, and said he would go home. I suggested a cab, but he replied that he would rather walk.

I met McQuae in the evening at the St. James's Theatre. It was a first night, and he was taking sketches for The Graphic. The moment he saw me he made his way across to me.

"The very man I wanted to see," he said. "Did I take Hallyard with me in the cart to Richmond this afternoon?"

"You did," I replied.

"So Leena says," he answered, greatly bewildered, "but I'll swear he wasn't there when we got to the Queen's Hotel."

"It's all right," I said, "you dropped him at Putney."

"Dropped him at Putney!" he repeated. "I've no recollection of doing so."

"He has," I answered. "You ask him about it. He's full of it."

Everybody said he never would get married; that it was absurd to suppose he ever would remember the day, the church, and the girl, all in one morning; that if he did get as far as the altar he would forget what he had come for, and would give the bride away to his own best man.

Hallyard had an idea that he was already married, but that the fact had slipped his memory. I myself felt sure that if he did marry he would forget all about it the next day.

But everybody was wrong. By some miraculous means the ceremony got itself accomplished, so that if Hallyard's idea be correct (as to which there is every possibility), there will be trouble. As for my own fears, I dismissed them the moment I saw the lady. She was a charming, cheerful little woman, but did not look the type that would let him forget all about it.

I had not seen him since his marriage, which had happened in the spring. Working my way back from Scotland by easy stages, I stopped for a few days at Scarboro'. After table d'hote I put on my mackintosh, and went out for a walk. It was raining hard, but after a month in Scotland one does not notice English weather, and I wanted some air. Struggling along the dark beach with my head against the wind, I stumbled over a crouching figure, seeking to shelter itself a little from the storm under the lee of the Spa wall.

I expected it to swear at me, but it seemed too broken-spirited to mind anything.

"I beg your pardon," I said. "I did not see you."

At the sound of my voice it started to its feet.

"Is that you, old man?" it cried.

"McQuae!" I exclaimed.

"By Jove!" he said, "I was never so glad to see a man in all my life before."

And he nearly shook my hand off.

"But what in thunder!" I said, "are you doing here? Why, you're drenched to the skin."

He was dressed in flannels and a tennis-coat.

"Yes," he answered. "I never thought it would rain. It was a lovely morning."

I began to fear he had overworked himself into a brain fever.

"Why don't you go home?" I asked.

"I can't," he replied. "I don't know where I live. I've forgotten the address."

"For heaven's sake," he said, "take me somewhere, and give me something to eat. I'm literally starving."

"Haven't you any money?" I asked him, as we turned towards the hotel.

"Not a sou," he answered. "We got in here from York, the wife and I, about eleven. We left our things at the station, and started to hunt for apartments. As soon as we were fixed, I changed my clothes and came out for a walk, telling Maud I should be back at one to lunch. Like a fool, I never took the address, and never noticed the way I was going.

"It's an awful business," he continued. "I don't see how I'm ever going to find her. I hoped she might stroll down to the Spa in the evening, and I've been hanging about the gates ever since six. I hadn't the threepence to go in."

"But have you no notion of the sort of street or the kind of house it was?" I enquired.

"Not a ghost," he replied. "I left it all to Maud, and didn't trouble."

"Have you tried any of the lodging-houses?" I asked.

"Tried!" he exclaimed bitterly. "I've been knocking at doors, and asking if Mrs. McQuae lives there steadily all the afternoon, and they slam the door in my face, mostly without answering. I told a policeman, I thought perhaps he might suggest something, but the idiot only burst out laughing, and that made me so mad that I gave him a black eye, and had to cut. I expect they're on the lookout for me now."

"I went into a restaurant," he continued gloomily, "and tried to get them to trust me for a steak. But the proprietress said she'd heard that tale before, and ordered me out before all the other customers. I think I'd have drowned myself if you hadn't turned up."

After a change of clothes and some supper, he discussed the case more calmly, but it was really a serious affair. They had shut up their flat, and his wife's relatives were travelling abroad.

There was no one to whom he could send a letter to be forwarded; there was no one with whom she would be likely to communicate. Their chance of meeting again in this world appeared remote.

7

Nor did it seem to me, fond as he was of his wife, and anxious as he undoubtedly was to recover her, that he looked forward to the actual meeting, should it ever arrive, with any too pleasurable anticipation.

"She will think it strange," he murmured reflectively, sitting on the edge of the bed, and thoughtfully pulling off his socks. "She is sure to think it strange."

The following day, which was Wednesday, we went to a solicitor, and laid the case before him, and he instituted inquiries among all the lodging-house keepers in Scarborough, with the result that on Thursday afternoon McQuae was restored (after the manner of an Adelphi hero in the last act) to his home and wife.

I asked him next time I met him what she had said.

"Oh, much what I expected," he replied.

But he never told me what he had expected.

The Cost of Kindness

"Kindness," argued little Mrs. Pennycoop, "costs nothing."

"And, speaking generally, my dear, is valued precisely at cost price," retorted Mr. Pennycoop, who, as an auctioneer of twenty years' experience, had enjoyed much opportunity of testing the attitude of the public towards sentiment.

"I don't care what you say, George," persisted his wife; "he may be a disagreeable, cantankerous old brute I don't say he isn't. All the same, the man is going away, and we may never see him again."

"If I thought there was any fear of our doing so," observed Mr. Pennycoop, "I'd turn my back on the Church of England to-morrow and become a Methodist."

"Don't talk like that, George," his wife admonished him, reprovingly; "the Lord might be listening to you."

"If the Lord had to listen to old Cracklethorpe He'd sympathize with me," was the opinion of Mr. Pennycoop.

"The Lord sends us our trials, and they are meant for our good," explained his wife. "They are meant to teach us patience."

"You are not churchwarden," retorted her husband; "you can get away from him. You hear him when he is in the pulpit, where, to a certain extent, he is bound to keep his temper."

"You forget the rummage sale, George," Mrs. Pennycoop reminded him; "to say nothing of the church decorations."

"The rummage sale," Mr. Pennycoop pointed out to her, "occurs only once a year, and at that time your own temper, I have noticed -"

"I always try to remember I am a Christian," interrupted little Mrs. Pennycoop. "I do not pretend to be a saint, but whatever I say I am always sorry for it afterwards, you know I am, George."

"It's what I am saying," explained her husband. "A vicar who has contrived in three years to make every member of his congregation hate the very sight of a church well, there's something wrong about it somewhere."

Mrs. Pennycoop, gentlest of little women, laid her plump and still pretty hands upon her husband's shoulders. "Don't think, dear, I haven't sympathized with you. You have borne it nobly. I have marvelled sometimes that you have been able to control yourself as you have done, most times; the things that he has said to you."

Mr. Pennycoop had slid unconsciously into an attitude suggestive of petrified virtue, lately discovered.

"One's own poor self," observed Mr. Pennycoop, in accents of proud humility--"insults that are merely personal one can put up with. Though even there," added the senior churchwarden, with momentary descent towards the plane of human nature, "nobody cares to have it hinted publicly across the vestry table that one has chosen to collect from the left side for the express purpose of artfully passing over one's own family."

"The children have always had their three-penny-bits ready waiting in their hands," explained Mrs. Pennycoop, indignantly.

"It's the sort of thing he says merely for the sake of making a disturbance," continued the senior churchwarden. "It's the things he does I draw the line at."

"The things he has done, you mean, dear," laughed the little woman, with the accent on the "has." "It is all over now, and we are going to be rid of him. I expect, dear, if we only knew, we should find it was his liver. You know, George, I remarked to you the first day that he came how pasty he looked and what a singularly unpleasant mouth he had. People can't help these things, you know, dear. One should look upon them in the light of afflictions and be sorry for them."

"I could forgive him doing what he does if he didn't seem to enjoy it," said the senior churchwarden. "But, as you say, dear, he is going, and all I hope and pray is that we never see his like again."

"And you'll come with me to call upon him, George," urged kind little Mrs. Pennycoop. "After all, he has been our vicar for three years, and he must be feeling it, poor man whatever he may pretend, going away like this, knowing that everybody is glad to see the back of him."

"Well, I sha'n't say anything I don't really feel," stipulated Mr. Pennycoop.

"That will be all right, dear," laughed his wife, "so long as you don't say what you do feel. And we'll both of us keep our temper," further suggested the little woman, "whatever happens. Remember, it will be for the last time."

Little Mrs. Pennycoop's intention was kind and Christianlike. The Rev. Augustus Cracklethorpe would be quitting Wychwood-on-the-Heath the following Monday, never to set foot so the Rev. Augustus Cracklethorpe himself and every single member of his congregation hoped sincerely in the neighbourhood again. Hitherto no pains had been taken on either side to disguise the mutual joy with which the parting was looked forward to. The Rev. Augustus Cracklethorpe, M.A., might possibly have been of service to his Church in, say, some East-end parish of unsavoury reputation, some mission station far advanced amid the hordes of heathendom. There his inborn instinct of antagonism to everybody and everything surrounding him, his unconquerable disregard for other people's views and feelings, his inspired conviction that everybody but himself was bound to be always wrong about everything, combined with determination to act and speak fearlessly in such belief, might have found their uses. In picturesque little Wychwood-on-the-Heath, among the Kentish hills, retreat beloved of the retired tradesman, the spinster of moderate means, the reformed Bohemian developing latent instincts towards respectability, these qualities made only for scandal and disunion.

For the past two years the Rev. Cracklethorpe's parishioners, assisted by such other of the inhabitants of Wychwood-on-the-Heath as had happened to come into personal contact with the reverend gentleman, had sought to impress upon him, by hints and innuendoes difficult to misunderstand, their cordial and daily-increasing dislike of him, both as a parson and a man. Matters had come to a head by the determination officially announced to him that, failing other alternatives, a deputation of his leading parishioners would wait upon his bishop. This it was that had brought it home to the Rev. Augustus Cracklethorpe that, as the spiritual guide and comforter of Wychwood-on-the Heath, he had proved a failure. The Rev. Augustus had sought and secured the care of other souls. The following Sunday morning he had arranged to preach his farewell sermon, and the occasion promised to be a success from every point of view. Churchgoers who had not visited St. Jude's for months had promised themselves the luxury of feeling they were listening to the Rev. Augustus Cracklethorpe for the last time. The Rev. Augustus Cracklethorpe had prepared a sermon that for plain speaking and directness was likely to leave an impression. The parishioners of St. Jude's, Wychwood-on-the-Heath, had their failings, as we all have. The Rev. Augustus flattered himself that he had not missed out a single one, and was looking forward with pleasurable anticipation to the sensation that his remarks, from his "firstly" to his "sixthly and lastly," were likely to create.

What marred the entire business was the impulsiveness of little Mrs. Pennycoop. The Rev. Augustus Cracklethorpe, informed in his study on the Wednesday afternoon that Mr. and Mrs. Pennycoop had called, entered the drawing-room a quarter of an hour later, cold and severe; and, without offering to shake hands, requested to be informed as shortly as possible for what purpose he had been disturbed. Mrs. Pennycoop had had her speech ready to her tongue. It was just what it should have been, and no more.

It referred casually, without insisting on the point, to the duty incumbent upon all of us to remember on occasion we were Christians; that our privilege it was to forgive and forget; that, generally speaking, there are faults on both sides; that partings should never take place in anger; in short, that little Mrs. Pennycoop and George, her husband, as he was waiting to say for himself, were sorry for everything and anything they may have said or done in the past to hurt the feelings of the Rev. Augustus Cracklethorpe, and would like to shake hands with him and wish him every happiness for the future. The chilling attitude of the Rev. Augustus scattered that carefully-rehearsed speech to the winds. It left Mrs. Pennycoop nothing but to retire in choking silence, or to fling herself upon the inspiration of the moment and make up something new. She choose the latter alternative.

At first the words came halting. Her husband, man-like, had deserted her in her hour of utmost need and was fumbling with the door-knob. The steely stare with which the Rev. Cracklethorpe regarded her, instead of chilling her, acted upon her as a spur.

It put her on her mettle. He should listen to her. She would make him understand her kindly feeling towards him if she had to take him by the shoulders and shake it into him. At the end of five minutes the Rev.

Augustus Cracklethorpe, without knowing it, was looking pleased. At the end of another five Mrs. Pennycoop stopped, not for want of words, but for want of breath. The Rev. Augustus Cracklethorpe replied in a voice that, to his own surprise, was trembling with emotion. Mrs. Pennycoop had made his task harder for him. He had thought to leave Wychwood-on-the-Heath without a regret. The knowledge he now possessed, that at all events one member of his congregation understood him, as Mrs. Pennycoop had proved to him she understood him, sympathized with him--the knowledge that at least one heart, and that heart Mrs. Pennycoop's, had warmed to him, would transform what he had looked forward to as a blessed relief into a lasting grief.

Mr. Pennycoop, carried away by his wife's eloquence, added a few halting words of his own. It appeared from Mr. Pennycoop's remarks that he had always regarded the Rev. Augustus Cracklethorpe as the vicar of his dreams, but misunderstandings in some unaccountable way will arise. The Rev. Augustus Cracklethorpe, it appeared, had always secretly respected Mr. Pennycoop. If at any time his spoken words might have conveyed the contrary impression, that must have arisen from the poverty of our language, which does not lend itself to subtle meanings.

Then following the suggestion of tea, Miss Cracklethorpe, sister to the Rev. Augustus, a lady whose likeness to her brother in all respects was startling, the only difference between them being that while he was clean-shaven she wore a slight moustache, was called down to grace the board. The visit was ended by Mrs. Pennycoop's remembrance that it was Wilhelmina's night for a hot bath.

"I said more than I intended to," admitted Mrs. Pennycoop to George, her husband, on the way home; "but he irritated me."

Rumour of the Pennycoops' visit flew through the parish. Other ladies felt it their duty to show to Mrs. Pennycoop that she was not the only Christian in Wychwood-on-the-Heath. Mrs. Pennycoop, it was feared, might be getting a swelled head over this matter. The Rev. Augustus, with pardonable pride, repeated some of the things that Mrs. Pennycoop had said to him. Mrs. Pennycoop was not to imagine herself the only person in Wychwood-on-the-Heath capable of generosity that cost nothing. Other ladies could say graceful nothings--could say them even better. Husbands dressed in their best clothes and carefully rehearsed were brought in to grace the almost endless procession of disconsolate parishioners hammering at the door of St. Jude's parsonage.

Between Thursday morning and Saturday night the Rev. Augustus, much to his own astonishment, had been forced to the conclusion that five-sixths of his parishioners had loved him from the first without hitherto having had opportunity of expressing their real feelings.

The eventful Sunday arrived. The Rev. Augustus Cracklethorpe had been kept so busy listening to regrets at his departure, assurances of an esteem hitherto disguised from him, explanations of seeming discourtesies that had been intended as tokens of affectionate regard, that no time had been left to him to think of other matters. Not till he entered the vestry at five minutes to eleven did recollection of his farewell sermon come to him. It haunted him throughout the service. To deliver it after the revelations of the last three days would be impossible. It was the sermon that Moses might have preached to Pharaoh the Sunday prior to the exodus. To crush with it this congregation of broken-hearted adorers sorrowing for his departure would be inhuman. The Rev. Augustus tried to think of passages that might be selected, altered. There were none. From beginning to end it contained not a single sentence capable of being made to sound pleasant by any ingenuity whatsoever.

The Rev. Augustus Cracklethorpe climbed slowly up the pulpit steps without an idea in his head of what he was going to say. The sunlight fell upon the upturned faces of a crowd that filled every corner of the church. So happy, so buoyant a congregation the eyes of the Rev. Augustus Cracklethorpe had never till that day looked down upon. The feeling came to him that he did not want to leave them. That they did not wish him to go, could he doubt? Only by regarding them as a collection of the most shameless hypocrites ever gathered together under one roof. The Rev. Augustus Cracklethorpe dismissed the passing suspicion as a suggestion of the Evil One, folded the neatly-written manuscript that lay before him on the desk, and put it aside. He had no need of a farewell sermon. The arrangements made could easily be altered. The Rev. Augustus Cracklethorpe spoke from his pulpit for the first time an impromptu.

The Rev. Augustus Cracklethorpe wished to acknowledge himself in the wrong. Foolishly founding his judgment upon the evidence of a few men, whose names there would be no need to mention, members of the congregation who, he hoped, would one day be sorry for the misunderstandings they had caused, brethren whom it was his duty to forgive, he had assumed the parishioners of St. Jude's, Wychwood-on-the-Heath, to have taken a personal dislike to him. He wished to publicly apologize for the injustice he had unwittingly done to their heads and to their hearts. He now had it from their own lips that a libel had been put upon them. So far from their wishing his departure, it was self-evident that his going would inflict upon them a great sorrow.

With the knowledge he now possessed of the respect - one might almost say the veneration - with which the majority of that congregation regarded him, knowledge, he admitted, acquired somewhat late, it was clear to him he could still be of help to them in their spiritual need. To leave a flock so devoted would stamp him as an unworthy shepherd. The ceaseless stream of regrets at his departure that had been poured into his ear during the last four days he had decided at the last moment to pay heed to. He would remain with them on one condition.

There quivered across the sea of humanity below him a movement that might have suggested to a more observant watcher the convulsive clutchings of some drowning man at some chance straw. But the Rev. Augustus Cracklethorpe was thinking of himself.

The parish was large and he was no longer a young man. Let them provide him with a conscientious and energetic curate. He had such a one in his mind's eye, a near relation of his own, who, for a small stipend that was hardly worth mentioning, would, he knew it for a fact, accept the post. The pulpit was not the place in which to discuss these matters, but in the vestry afterwards he would be pleased to meet such members of the congregation as might choose to stay.

The question agitating the majority of the congregation during the singing of the hymn was the time it would take them to get outside the church. There still remained a faint hope that the Rev. Augustus Cracklethorpe, not obtaining his curate, might consider it due to his own dignity to shake from his feet the dust of a parish generous in sentiment, but obstinately close-fisted when it came to putting its hands into its pockets.

But for the parishioners of St. Jude's that Sunday was a day of misfortune. Before there could be any thought of moving, the Rev. Augustus raised his surpliced arm and begged leave to acquaint them with the contents of a short note that had just been handed up to him. It would send them all home, he felt sure, with joy and thankfulness in their hearts. An example of Christian benevolence was among them that did honour to the Church.

Here a retired wholesale clothier from the East-end of London, a short, tubby gentleman who had recently taken the Manor House, was observed to turn scarlet.

A gentleman hitherto unknown to them had signalled his advent among them by an act of munificence that should prove a shining example to all rich men. Mr. Horatio Copper the reverend gentleman found some difficulty, apparently, in deciphering the name.

"Cooper-Smith, sir, with an hyphen," came in a thin whisper, the voice of the still scarlet-faced clothier.

Mr. Horatio Cooper-Smith, taking - the Rev. Augustus felt confident - a not unworthy means of grappling to himself thus early the hearts of his fellow-townsmen, had expressed his desire to pay for the expense of a curate entirely out of his own pocket. Under these circumstances, there would be no further talk of a farewell between the Rev. Augustus Cracklethorpe and his parishioners. It would be the hope of the Rev. Augustus Cracklethorpe to live and die the pastor of St. Jude's.

A more solemn-looking, sober congregation than the congregation that emerged that Sunday morning from St. Jude's in Wychwood-on-the-Heath had never, perhaps, passed out of a church door.

"He'll have more time upon his hands," said Mr. Biles, retired wholesale ironmonger and junior churchwarden, to Mrs. Biles, turning the corner of Acacia Avenue "he'll have more time to make himself a curse and a stumbling-block."

"And if this 'near relation' of his is anything like him -"

"Which you may depend upon it is the Case, or he'd never have thought of him," was the opinion of Mr. Biles.

"I shall give that Mrs. Pennycoop," said Mrs. Biles, "a piece of my mind when I meet her."

But of what use was that?

The Lesson

The first time I met him, to my knowledge, was on an evil-smelling, one-funnelled steam boat that in those days plied between London Bridge and Antwerp. He was walking the deck arm-in-arm with a showily dressed but decidedly attractive young woman; both of them talking and laughing loudly. It struck me as odd, finding him a fellow-traveller by such a route. The passage occupied eighteen hours, and the first-class return fare was one pound twelve and six, including three meals each way; drinks, as the contract was careful to explain, being extra. I was earning thirty shillings a week at the time as clerk with a firm of agents in Fenchurch Street. Our business was the purchasing of articles on commission for customers in India, and I had learned to be a judge of values. The beaver lined coat he was wearing--for the evening, although it was late summer, was chilly--must have cost him a couple of hundred pounds, while his carelessly displayed jewellery he could easily have pawned for a thousand or more. I could not help staring at him, and once, as they passed, he returned my look.

After dinner, as I was leaning with my back against the gunwale on the starboard side, he came out of the only private cabin that the vessel boasted, and taking up a position opposite to me, with his legs well apart and a big cigar between his thick lips, stood coolly regarding me, as if appraising me.

"Treating yourself to a little holiday on the Continent?" he inquired.

I had not been quite sure before he spoke, but his lisp, though slight, betrayed the Jew. His features were coarse, almost brutal; but the restless eyes were so brilliant, the whole face so suggestive of power and character, that, taking him as a whole, the feeling he inspired was admiration, tempered by fear. His tone was one of kindly contempt--the tone of a man accustomed to find most people his inferiors, and too used to the discovery to be conceited about it.

Behind it was a note of authority that it did not occur to me to dispute.

"Yes," I answered, adding the information that I had never been abroad before, and had heard that Antwerp was an interesting town.

"How long have you got?" he asked.

"A fortnight," I told him.

"Like to see a bit more than Antwerp, if you could afford it, wouldn't you?" he suggested. "Fascinating little country Holland. Just long enough--a fortnight--to do the whole of it. I'm a Dutchman, a Dutch Jew."

"You speak English just like an Englishman," I told him. It was somehow in my mind to please him. I could hardly have explained why.

"And half a dozen other languages equally well," he answered, laughing. "I left Amsterdam when I was eighteen as steerage passenger in an emigrant ship. I haven't seen it since."

He closed the cabin door behind him, and, crossing over, laid a strong hand on my shoulder.

"I will make a proposal to you," he said. "My business is not of the kind that can be put out of mind, even for a few days, and there are reasons" he glanced over his shoulder towards the cabin door, and gave vent to a short laugh "why I did not want to bring any of my own staff with me. If you care for a short tour, all expenses paid at slap-up hotels and a ten-pound note in your pocket at the end, you can have it for two hours' work a day."

I suppose my face expressed my acceptance, for he did not wait for me to speak.

"Only one thing I stipulate for," he added, "that you mind your own business and keep your mouth shut. You're by yourself, aren't you?"

"Yes," I told him.

He wrote on a sheet of his notebook, and, tearing it out, handed it to me.

"That's your hotel at Antwerp," he said. "You are Mr. Horatio Jones's secretary." He chuckled to himself as he repeated the name, which certainly did not fit him. "Knock at my sitting-room door at nine o'clock tomorrow morning. Good night!"

He ended the conversation as abruptly as he had begun it, and returned to his cabin.

I got a glimpse of him next morning, coming out of the hotel bureau. He was speaking to the manager in French, and had evidently given instructions concerning me, for I found myself preceded by an obsequious waiter to quite a charming bedroom on the second floor, while the "English breakfast" placed before me later in the coffee-room was of a size and character that in those days I did not often enjoy. About the work, also, he was as good as his word. I was rarely occupied for more than two hours each morning. The duties consisted chiefly of writing letters and sending off telegrams. The letters he signed and had posted himself, so that I never learnt his real name, not during that fortnight, but I gathered enough to be aware that he was a man whose business interests must have been colossal and world-wide.

He never introduced me to "Mrs. Horatio Jones," and after a few days he seemed to be bored with her, so that often I would take her place as his companion in afternoon excursions.

I could not help liking the man. Strength always compels the adoration of youth; and there was something big and heroic about him. His daring, his swift decisions, his utter unscrupulousness, his occasional cruelty when necessity seemed to demand it.

One could imagine him in earlier days a born leader of savage hordes, a lover of fighting for its own sake, meeting all obstacles with fierce welcome, forcing his way onward, indifferent to the misery and destruction caused by his progress, his eyes never swerving from their goal; yet not without a sense of rough justice, not altogether without kindliness when it could be indulged in without danger.

One afternoon he took me with him into the Jewish quarter of Amsterdam, and threading his way without hesitation through its maze of unsavoury slums, paused before a narrow three-storeyed house overlooking a stagnant backwater.

"The room I was born in," he explained. "Window with the broken pane on the second floor. It has never been mended."

I stole a glance at him. His face betrayed no suggestion of sentiment, but rather of amusement. He offered me a cigar, which I was glad of, for the stench from the offal-laden water behind us was distracting, and for a while we both smoked in silence: he with his eyes half-closed; it was a trick of his when working out a business problem.

"Curious, my making such a choice," he remarked. "A butcher's assistant for my father and a consumptive buttonhole-maker for my mother. I suppose I knew what I was about. Quite the right thing for me to have done, as it turned out."

I stared at him, wondering whether he was speaking seriously or in grim jest. He was given at times to making odd remarks. There was a vein of the fantastic in him that was continually cropping out and astonishing me.

"It was a bit risky," I suggested. "Better choose something a little safer next time."

He looked round at me sharply, and, not quite sure of his mood, I kept a grave face.

"Perhaps you are right," he agreed, with a laugh. "We must have a talk about it one day."

After that visit to the Goortgasse he was less reserved with me, and would often talk to me on subjects that I should never have guessed would have interested him. I found him a curious mixture. Behind the shrewd, cynical man of business I caught continual glimpses of the visionary.

I parted from him at The Hague. He paid my fare back to London, and gave me an extra pound for travelling expenses, together with the ten-pound note he had promised me. He had packed off "Mrs. Horatio Jones" some days before, to the relief, I imagine, of both of them, and he himself continued his journey to Berlin. I never expected to see him again, although for the next few months I often thought of him, and even tried to discover him by inquiries in the City. I had, however, very little to go upon, and after I had left Fenchurch Street behind me, and drifted into literature, I forgot him.

Until one day I received a letter addressed to the care of my publishers. It bore the Swiss postmark, and opening it and turning to the signature I sat wondering for the moment where I had met "Horatio Jones." And then I remembered.

He was lying bruised and broken in a woodcutter's hut on the slopes of the Jungfrau. Had been playing a fool's trick, so he described it, thinking he could climb mountains at his age. They would carry him down to Lauterbrunnen as soon as he could be moved farther with safety, but for the present he had no one to talk to but the nurse and a Swiss doctor who climbed up to see him every third day. He begged me, if I could spare the time, to come over and spend a week with him. He enclosed a hundred-pound cheque for my expenses, making no apology for doing so. He was complimentary about my first book, which he had been reading, and asked me to telegraph him my reply, giving me his real name, which, as I had guessed it would, proved to be one of the best known in the financial world. My time was my own now, and I wired him that I would be with him the following Monday.

He was lying in the sun outside the hut when I arrived late in the afternoon, after a three-hours' climb followed by a porter carrying my small amount of luggage. He could not raise his hand, but his strangely brilliant eyes spoke their welcome.

"I am glad you were able to come," he said. "I have no near relations, and my friends, if that is the right term, are business men who would be bored to tears. Besides, they are not the people I feel I want to talk to, now."

He was entirely reconciled to the coming of death. Indeed, there were moments when he gave me the idea that he was looking forward to it with an awed curiosity. With the conventional notion of cheering him, I talked of staying till he was able to return with me to civilisation, but he only laughed.

"I am not going back," he said. "Not that way. What they may do afterwards with these broken bones does not much concern either you or me.

"It's a good place to die in," he continued. "A man can think up here."

It was difficult to feel sorry for him, his own fate appearing to make so little difference to himself. The world was still full of interest to him - not his own particular corner of it: that, he gave me to understand, he had tidied up and dismissed from his mind. It was the future, its coming problems, its possibilities, its new developments, about which he seemed eager to talk. One might have imagined him a young man with the years before him.

One evening, it was near the end, we were alone together. The woodcutter and his wife had gone down into the valley to see their children, and the nurse, leaving him in my charge, had gone for a walk. We had carried him round to his favourite side of the hut facing the towering mass of the Jungfrau. As the shadows lengthened it seemed to come nearer to us, and there fell a silence upon us.

Gradually I became aware that his piercing eyes were fixed on me, and in answer I turned and looked at him.

"I wonder if we shall meet again," he said, "or, what is more important, if we shall remember one another."

I was puzzled for the moment. We had discussed more than once the various religions of mankind, and his attitude towards the orthodox beliefs had always been that of amused contempt.

"It has been growing upon me these last few days," he continued. "It flashed across me the first time I saw you on the boat. We were fellow-students. Something, I don't know what, drew us very close together. There was a woman. They were burning her. And then there was a rush of people and a sudden darkness, and your eyes close to mine."

I suppose it was some form of hypnotism, for, as he spoke, his searching eyes fixed on mine, there came to me a dream of narrow streets filled with a strange crowd, of painted houses such as I had never seen, and a haunting fear that seemed to be always lurking behind each shadow. I shook myself free, but not without an effort.

"So that's what you meant," I said, "that evening in the Goortgasse. You believe in it?"

"A curious thing happened to me," he said, "when I was a child. I could hardly have been six years old. I had gone to Ghent with my parents. I think it was to visit some relative. One day we went into the castle. It was in ruins then, but has since been restored. We were in what was once the council chamber. I stole away by myself to the other end of the great room and, not knowing why I did so, I touched a spring concealed in the masonry, and a door swung open with a harsh, grinding noise. I remember peering round the opening. The others had their backs towards me, and I slipped through and closed the door behind me. I seemed instinctively to know my way. I ran down a flight of steps and along dark corridors through which I had to feel my way with my hands, till I came to a small door in an angle of the wall. I knew the room that lay the other side. A photograph was taken of it and published years afterwards, when the place was discovered, and it was exactly as I knew it with its way out underneath the city wall through one of the small houses in the Aussermarkt.

"I could not open the door. Some stones had fallen against it, and fearing to get punished, I made my way back into the council room. It was empty when I reached it. They were searching for me in the other rooms, and I never told them of my adventure."

At any other time I might have laughed. Later, recalling his talk that evening, I dismissed the whole story as mere suggestion, based upon the imagination of a child; but at the time those strangely brilliant eyes had taken possession of me. They remained still fixed upon me as I sat on the low rail of the veranda watching his white face, into which the hues of death seemed already to be creeping.

I had a feeling that, through them, he was trying to force remembrance of himself upon me. The man himself, the very soul of him, seemed to be concentrated in them. Something formless and yet distinct was visualising itself before me. It came to me as a physical relief when a spasm of pain caused him to turn his eyes away from me.

"You will find a letter when I am gone," he went on, after a moment's silence. "I thought that you might come too late, or that I might not have strength enough to tell you. I felt that out of the few people I have met outside business, you would be the most likely not to dismiss the matter as mere nonsense. What I am glad of myself, and what I wish you to remember, is that I am dying with all my faculties about me. The one thing I have always feared through life was old age, with its gradual mental decay. It has always seemed to me that I have died more or less suddenly while still in possession of my will. I have always thanked God for that."

He closed his eyes, but I do not think he was sleeping; and a little later the nurse returned, and we carried him indoors. I had no further conversation with him, though at his wish during the following two days I continued to read to him, and on the third day he died.

I found the letter he had spoken of. He had told me where it would be. It contained a bundle of banknotes which he was giving me, so he wrote, with the advice to get rid of them as quickly as possible.

"If I had not loved you," the letter continued, "I would have left you an income, and you would have blessed me, instead of cursing me, as you should have done, for spoiling your life."

21

This world was a school, so he viewed it, for the making of men; and the one thing essential to a man was strength. One gathered the impression of a deeply religious man. In these days he would, no doubt, have been claimed as a theosophist; but his beliefs he had made for, and adapted to, himself to his vehement, conquering temperament. God needed men to serve Him, to help Him. So, through many changes, through many ages, God gave men life: that by contest and by struggle they might ever increase in strength; to those who proved themselves most fit the sterner task, the humbler beginnings, the greater obstacles. And the crown of well-doing was ever victory. He appeared to have convinced himself that he was one of the chosen, that he was destined for great ends. He had been a slave in the time of the Pharaohs; a priest in Babylon; had clung to the swaying ladders in the sack of Rome; had won his way into the councils when Europe was a battlefield of contending tribes; had climbed to power in the days of the Borgias.

To most of us, I suppose, there come at odd moments haunting thoughts of strangely familiar, far-off things; and one wonders whether they are memories or dreams. We dismiss them as we grow older and the present with its crowding interests shuts them out; but in youth they were more persistent. With him they appeared to have remained, growing in reality. His recent existence, closed under the white sheet in the hut behind me as I read, was only one chapter of the story; he was looking forward to the next.

He wondered, so the letter ran, whether he would have any voice in choosing it. In either event he was curious of the result. What he anticipated confidently were new opportunities, wider experience. In what shape would these come to him?

The letter ended with a strange request.

It was that, on returning to England, I should continue to think of him: not of the dead man I had known, the Jewish banker, the voice familiar to me, the trick of speech, of manner all such being but the changing clothes but of the man himself, the soul of him, that would seek and perhaps succeed in revealing itself to me.

A postscript concluded the letter, to which at the time I attached no importance. He had made a purchase of the hut in which he had died. After his removal it was to remain empty.

I folded the letter and placed it among other papers, and passing into the hut took a farewell glance at the massive, rugged face. The mask might have served a sculptor for the embodiment of strength. He gave one the feeling that having conquered death he was sleeping.

I did what he had requested of me. Indeed, I could not help it. I thought of him constantly. That may have been the explanation of it.

I was bicycling through Norfolk, and one afternoon, to escape a coming thunderstorm, I knocked at the door of a lonely cottage on the outskirts of a common. The woman, a kindly bustling person, asked me in; and hoping I would excuse her, as she was busy ironing, returned to her work in another room. I thought myself alone, and was standing at the window watching the pouring rain. After a while, without knowing why, I turned. And then I saw a child seated on a high chair behind a table in a dark corner of the room. A book of pictures was open before it, but it was looking at me. I could hear the sound of the woman at her ironing in the other room. Outside there was the steady thrashing of the rain. The child was looking at me with large, round eyes filled with a terrible pathos. I noticed that the little body was misshapen. It never moved; it made no sound; but I had the feeling that out of those strangely wistful eyes something was trying to speak to me. Something was forming itself before me--not visible to my sight; but it was there, in the room. It was the man I had last looked upon as, dying, he sat beside me in the hut below the Jungfrau. But something had happened to him. Moved by instinct I went over to him and lifted him out of his chair, and with a sob the little wizened arms closed round my neck and he clung to me crying a pitiful, low, wailing cry.

Hearing his cry, the woman came back. A comely, healthy-looking woman. She took him from my arms and comforted him.

"He gets a bit sorry for himself at times," she explained. "At least, so I fancy. You see, he can't run about like other children, or do anything without getting pains."

"Was it an accident?" I asked.

"No," she answered, "and his father as fine a man as you would find in a day's march. Just a visitation of God, as they tell me. Sure I don't know why. There never was a better little lad, and clever, too, when he's not in pain. Draws wonderfully."

The storm had passed. He grew quieter in her arms, and when I had promised to come again and bring him a new picture-book, a little grateful smile flickered across the drawn face, but he would not talk.

I kept in touch with him. Mere curiosity would have made me do that. He grew more normal as the years went by, and gradually the fancy that had come to me at our first meeting faded farther into the background. Sometimes, using the very language of the dead man's letter, I would talk to him, wondering if by any chance some flash of memory would come back to him, and once or twice it seemed to me that into the mild, pathetic eyes there came a look that I had seen before, but it passed away, and indeed, it was difficult to think of this sad little human oddity, with its pleading helplessness, in connection with the strong, swift, conquering spirit that I had watched passing away amid the silence of the mountains.

The one thing that brought joy to him was his art. I cannot help thinking that, but for his health, he would have made a name for himself. His work was always clever and original, but it was the work of an invalid.

"I shall never be great," he said to me once. "I have such wonderful dreams, but when it comes to working them out there is something that hampers me. It always seems to me as if at the last moment a hand was stretched out that clutched me by the feet. I long so, but I have not the strength. It is terrible to be one of the weaklings."

It clung to me, that word he had used. For a man to know he is weak; it sounds a paradox, but a man must be strong to know that. And dwelling upon this, and upon his patience and his gentleness, there came to me suddenly remembrance of that postscript, the significance of which I had not understood.

He was a young man of about three- or four-and-twenty at the time. His father had died, and he was living in poor lodgings in the south of London, supporting himself and his mother by strenuous, ill-paid work.

"I want you to come with me for a few days' holiday," I told him.

I had some difficulty in getting him to accept my help, for he was very proud in his sensitive, apologetic way. But I succeeded eventually, persuading him it would be good for his work.
Physically the journey must have cost him dear, for he could never move his body without pain, but the changing landscapes and the strange cities more than repaid him; and when one morning I woke him early and he saw for the first time the distant mountains clothed in dawn, there came a new light into his eyes.

We reached the hut late in the afternoon. I had made my arrangements so that we should be there alone. Our needs were simple, and in various wanderings I had learnt to be independent. I did not tell him why I had brought him there, beyond the beauty and stillness of the place.
Purposely I left him much alone there, making ever-lengthening walks my excuse, and though he was always glad of my return I felt that the desire was growing upon him to be there by himself.

One evening, having climbed farther than I had intended, I lost my way. It was not safe in that neighbourhood to try new pathways in the dark, and chancing upon a deserted shelter, I made myself a bed upon the straw.

I found him seated outside the hut when I returned, and he greeted me as if he had been expecting me just at that moment and not before. He guessed just what had happened, he told me, and had not been alarmed. During the day I found him watching me, and in the evening, as we sat in his favourite place outside the hut, he turned to me.

"You think it true?" he said. "That you and I sat here years ago and talked?"

"I cannot tell," I answered. "I only know that he died here, if there be such a thing as death that no one has ever lived here since. I doubt if the door has ever been opened till we came."

"They have always been with me," he continued, "these dreams. But I have always dismissed them. They seemed so ludicrous. Always there came to me wealth, power, victory. Life was so easy."

He laid his thin hand on mine. A strange new look came into his eyes a look of hope, almost of joy.

"Do you know what it seems to me?" he said. "You will laugh perhaps, but the thought has come to me up here that God has some fine use for me. Success was making me feeble. He has given me weakness and failure that I may learn strength. The great thing is to be strong."

A Man Of Habit

There were three of us in the smoke-room of the Alexandra, a very good friend of mine, myself, and, in the opposite corner, a shy-looking, unobtrusive man, the editor, as we subsequently learned, of a New York Sunday paper.

My friend and I were discussing habits, good and bad.

"After the first few months," said my friend, "it is no more effort for a man to be a saint than to be a sinner; it becomes a mere matter of habit."

"I know," I interrupted, "it is every whit as easy to spring out of bed the instant you are called as to say 'All Right,' and turn over for just another five minutes' snooze, when you have got into the way of it. It is no more trouble not to swear than to swear, if you make a custom of it. Toast and water is as delicious as champagne, when you have acquired the taste for it. Things are also just as easy the other way about. It is a mere question of making your choice and sticking to it."

He agreed with me.

"Now take these cigars of mine," he said, pushing his open case towards me.

"Thank you," I replied hurriedly, "I'm not smoking this passage."

"Don't be alarmed," he answered, "I meant merely as an argument. Now one of these would make you wretched for a week."

I admitted his premise.

"Very well," he continued. "Now I, as you know, smoke them all day long, and enjoy them. Why? Because I have got into the habit. Years ago, when I was a young man, I smoked expensive Havanas. I found that I was ruining myself. It was absolutely necessary that I should take a cheaper weed. I was living in Belgium at the time, and a friend showed me these. I don't know what they are probably cabbage leaves soaked in guano; they tasted to me like that at first but they were cheap. Buying them by the five hundred, they cost me three a penny. I determined to like them, and started with one a day. It was terrible work, I admit, but as I said to myself, nothing could be worse than the Havanas themselves had been in the beginning. Smoking is an acquired taste, and it must be as easy to learn to like one flavour as another. I persevered and I conquered.

Before the year was over I could think of them without loathing, at the end of two I could smoke them without positive discomfort. Now I prefer them to any other brand on the market. Indeed, a good cigar disagrees with me."

I suggested it might have been less painful to have given up smoking altogether.

"I did think of it," he replied, "but a man who doesn't smoke always seems to me bad company. There is something very sociable about smoke."

He leant back and puffed great clouds into the air, filling the small den with an odour suggestive of bilge water and cemeteries.

"Then again," he resumed after a pause, "take my claret. No, you don't like it." (I had not spoken, but my face had evidently betrayed me.)

"Nobody does, at least no one I have ever met. Three years ago, when I was living in Hammersmith, we caught two burglars with it. They broke open the sideboard, and swallowed five bottlefuls between them. A policeman found them afterwards, sitting on a doorstep a hundred yards off, the 'swag' beside them in a carpet bag. They were too ill to offer any resistance, and went to the station like lambs, he promising to send the doctor to them the moment they were safe in the cells. Ever since then I have left out a decanterful upon the table every night.

"Well, I like that claret, and it does me good. I come in sometimes dead beat. I drink a couple of glasses, and I'm a new man. I took to it in the first instance for the same reason that I took to the cigars, it was cheap. I have it sent over direct from Geneva, and it costs me six shillings a dozen. How they do it I don't know. I don't want to know. As you may remember, it's fairly heady and there's body in it.

"I knew one man," he continued, "who had a regular Mrs. Caudle of a wife. All day long she talked to him, or at him, or of him, and at night he fell asleep to the rising and falling rhythm of what she thought about him. At last she died, and his friends congratulated him, telling him that now he would enjoy peace. But it was the peace of the desert, and the man did not enjoy it. For two-and-twenty years her voice had filled the house, penetrated through the conservatory, and floated in faint shrilly waves of sound round the garden, and out into the road beyond. The silence now pervading everywhere frightened and disturbed him. The place was no longer home to him. He missed the breezy morning insult, the long winter evening's reproaches beside the flickering fire. At night he could not sleep. For hours he would lie tossing restlessly, his ears aching for the accustomed soothing flow of invective.

"'Ah!' he would cry bitterly to himself, 'it is the old story, we never know the value of a thing until we have lost it.'

"He grew ill. The doctors dosed him with sleeping draughts in vain. At last they told him bluntly that his life depended upon his finding another wife, able and willing to nag him to sleep.

"There were plenty of wives of the type he wanted in the neighbourhood, but the unmarried women were, of necessity, inexperienced, and his health was such that he could not afford the time to train them.

"Fortunately, just as despair was about to take possession of him, a man died in the next parish, literally talked to death, the gossip said, by his wife. He obtained an introduction, and called upon her the day after the funeral. She was a cantankerous old woman, and the wooing was a harassing affair, but his heart was in his work, and before six months were gone he had won her for his own.

"She proved, however, but a poor substitute. The spirit was willing but the flesh was weak. She had neither that command of language nor of wind that had distinguished her rival. From his favourite seat at the bottom of the garden he could not hear her at all, so he had his chair brought up into the conservatory. It was all right for him there so long as she continued to abuse him; but every now and again, just as he was getting comfortably settled down with his pipe and his newspaper, she would suddenly stop.

"He would drop his paper and sit listening, with a troubled, anxious expression.

"'Are you there, dear?' he would call out after a while.

"'Yes, I'm here. Where do you think I am you old fool?' she would gasp back in an exhausted voice.

"His face would brighten at the sound of her words. 'Go on, dear,' he would answer. 'I'm listening. I like to hear you talk.'

"But the poor woman was utterly pumped out, and had not so much as a snort left.

"Then he would shake his head sadly. 'No, she hasn't poor dear Susan's flow,' he would say. 'Ah! what a woman that was!'

"At night she would do her best, but it was a lame and halting performance by comparison.
After rating him for little over three-quarters of an hour, she would sink back on the pillow, and want to go to sleep. But he would shake her gently by the shoulder.

"'Yes, dear,' he would say, 'you were speaking about Jane, and the way I kept looking at her during lunch.'

"It's extraordinary," concluded my friend, lighting a fresh cigar, "what creatures of habit we are."

"Very," I replied. "I knew a man who told tall stories till when he told a true one nobody believed it."

"Ah, that was a very sad case," said my friend.

"Speaking of habit," said the unobtrusive man in the corner, "I can tell you a true story that I'll bet my bottom dollar you won't believe."

"Haven't got a bottom dollar, but I'll bet you half a sovereign I do," replied my friend, who was of a sporting turn. "Who shall be judge?"

"I'll take your word for it," said the unobtrusive man, and started straight away.

"He was a Jefferson man, this man I'm going to tell you of," he begun. "He was born in the town, and for forty-seven years he never slept a night outside it. He was a most respectable man, a drysalter from nine to four, and a Presbyterian in his leisure moments. He said that a good life merely meant good habits. He rose at seven, had family prayer at seven-thirty, breakfasted at eight, got to his business at nine, had his horse brought round to the office at four, and rode for an hour, reached home at five, had a bath and a cup of tea, played with and read to the children (he was a domesticated man) till half-past six, dressed and dined at seven, went round to the club and played whist till quarter after ten, home again to evening prayer at ten-thirty, and bed at eleven. For five-and-twenty years he lived that life with never a variation. It worked into his system and became mechanical. The church clocks were set by him. He was used by the local astronomers to check the sun.

"One day a distant connection of his in London, an East Indian Merchant and an ex-Lord Mayor died, leaving him sole legatee and executor. The business was a complicated one and needed management. He determined to leave his son by his first wife, now a young man of twenty-four, in charge at Jefferson, and to establish himself with his second family in England, and look after the East Indian business.

"He set out from Jefferson City on October the fourth, and arrived in London on the seventeenth. He had been ill during the whole of the voyage, and he reached the furnished house he had hired in Bayswater somewhat of a wreck. A couple of days in bed, however, pulled him round, and on the Wednesday evening he announced his intention of going into the City the next day to see to his affairs.

"On the Thursday morning he awoke at one o'clock. His wife told him she had not disturbed him, thinking the sleep would do him good. He admitted that perhaps it had. Anyhow, he felt very well, and he got up and dressed himself. He said he did not like the idea of beginning his first day by neglecting a religious duty, and his wife agreeing with him, they assembled the servants and the children in the dining-room, and had family prayer at half-past one. After which he breakfasted and set off, reaching the City about three.

"His reputation for punctuality had preceded him, and surprise was everywhere expressed at his late arrival. He explained the circumstances, however, and made his appointments for the following day to commence from nine-thirty.

"He remained at the office until late, and then went home. For dinner, usually the chief meal of the day, he could manage to eat only a biscuit and some fruit. He attributed his loss of appetite to want of his customary ride. He was strangely unsettled all the evening. He said he supposed he missed his game of whist, and determined to look about him without loss of time for some quiet, respectable club. At eleven he retired with his wife to bed, but could not sleep. He tossed and turned, and turned and tossed, but grew only more and more wakeful and energetic. A little after midnight an overpowering desire seized him to go and wish the children good-night. He slipped on a dressing-gown and stole into the nursery. He did not intend it, but the opening of the door awoke them, and he was glad. He wrapped them up in the quilt, and, sitting on the edge of the bed, told them moral stories till one o'clock.

"Then he kissed them, bidding them be good and go to sleep; and finding himself painfully hungry, crept downstairs, where in the back kitchen he made a hearty meal off cold game pie and cucumber.

"He retired to bed feeling more peaceful, yet still could not sleep, so lay thinking about his business affairs till five, when he dropped off.

"At one o'clock to the minute he awoke. His wife told him she had made every endeavour to rouse him, but in vain. The man was vexed and irritated.

If he had not been a very good man indeed, I believe he would have sworn. The same programme was repeated as on the Thursday, and again he reached the City at three.

"This state of things went on for a month. The man fought against himself, but was unable to alter himself. Every morning, or rather every afternoon at one he awoke. Every night at one he crept down into the kitchen and foraged for food. Every morning at five he fell asleep.

"He could not understand it, nobody could understand it. The doctor treated him for water on the brain, hypnotic irresponsibility and hereditary lunacy. Meanwhile his business suffered, and his health grew worse. He seemed to be living upside down. His days seemed to have neither beginning nor end, but to be all middle. There was no time for exercise or recreation. When he began to feel cheerful and sociable everybody else was asleep.

"One day by chance the explanation came. His eldest daughter was preparing her home studies after dinner.

"'What time is it now in New York?' she asked, looking up from her geography book.

"'New York,' said her father, glancing at his watch, 'let me see. It's just ten now, and there's a little over four and a half hours' difference. Oh, about half-past five in the afternoon.'

"'Then in Jefferson,' said the mother, 'it would be still earlier, wouldn't it?'

"'Yes,' replied the girl, examining the map, 'Jefferson is nearly two degrees further west.'

"'Two degrees,' mused the father, 'and there's forty minutes to a degree. That would make it now, at the present moment in Jefferson'

"He leaped to his feet with a cry:

"'I've got it!' he shouted, 'I see it.'

"'See what?' asked his wife, alarmed.

"'Why, it's four o'clock in Jefferson, and just time for my ride. That's what I'm wanting.'

"There could be no doubt about it. For five-and-twenty years he had lived by clockwork. But it was by Jefferson clockwork, not London clockwork. He had changed his longitude, but not himself. The habits of a quarter of a century were not to be shifted at the bidding of the sun.

"He examined the problem in all its bearings, and decided that the only solution was for him to return to the order of his old life. He saw the difficulties in his way, but they were less than those he was at present encountering. He was too formed by habit to adapt himself to circumstances. Circumstances must adapt themselves to him.

"He fixed his office hours from three till ten, leaving himself at half- past nine. At ten he mounted his horse and went for a canter in the Row, and on very dark nights he carried a lantern. News of it got abroad, and crowds would assemble to see him ride past.

"He dined at one o'clock in the morning, and afterwards strolled down to his club. He had tried to discover a quiet, respectable club where the members were willing to play whist till four in the morning, but failing, had been compelled to join a small Soho gambling-hell, where they taught him poker. The place was occasionally raided by the police, but thanks to his respectable appearance, he generally managed to escape.

"At half-past four he returned home, and woke up the family for evening prayers. At five he went to bed and slept like a top.

"The City chaffed him, and Bayswater shook its head over him, but that he did not mind. The only thing that really troubled him was loss of spiritual communion. At five o'clock on Sunday afternoons he felt he wanted chapel, but had to do without it. At seven he ate his simple mid-day meal. At eleven he had tea and muffins, and at midnight he began to crave again for hymns and sermons. At three he had a bread-and-cheese supper, and retired early at four a.m., feeling sad and unsatisfied.

"He was essentially a man of habit."

The unobtrusive stranger ceased, and we sat gazing in silence at the ceiling.

At length my friend rose, and taking half-a-sovereign from his pocket, laid it upon the table, and linking his arm in mine went out with me upon the deck.

The Man Who Went Wrong

I first met Jack Burridge nearly ten years ago on a certain North-country race-course.

The saddling bell had just rung for the chief event of the day. I was sauntering along with my hands in my pockets, more interested in the crowd than in the race, when a sporting friend, crossing on his way to the paddock, seized me by the arm and whispered hoarsely in my ear:--

"Put your shirt on Mrs. Waller."

"Put my -?" I began.

"Put your shirt on Mrs. Waller," he repeated still more impressively, and disappeared in the throng.

I stared after him in blank amazement. Why should I put my shirt on Mrs. Waller? Even if it would fit a lady. And how about myself?

I was passing the grand stand, and, glancing up, I saw "Mrs. Waller, twelve to one," chalked on a bookmaker's board. Then it dawned upon me that "Mrs. Waller" was a horse, and, thinking further upon the matter, I evolved the idea that my friend's advice, expressed in more becoming language, was "Back 'Mrs. Waller' for as much as you can possibly afford."

"Thank you," I said to myself, "I have backed cast-iron certainties before. Next time I bet upon a horse I shall make the selection by shutting my eyes and putting a pin through the card."

But the seed had taken root. My friend's words surged in my brain. The birds passing overhead twittered, "Put your shirt on 'Mrs. Waller.'"

I reasoned with myself. I reminded myself of my few former ventures. But the craving to put, if not my shirt, at all events half a sovereign on "Mrs. Waller" only grew the stronger the more strongly I battled against it. I felt that if "Mrs. Waller" won and I had nothing on her, I should reproach myself to my dying day.

I was on the other side of the course. There was no time to get back to the enclosure. The horses were already forming for the start. A few yards off, under a white umbrella, an outside bookmaker was shouting his final prices in stentorian tones. He was a big, genial-looking man, with an honest red face.

"What price 'Mrs. Waller'?" I asked him.

"Fourteen to one," he answered, "and good luck to you."

I handed him half a sovereign, and he wrote me out a ticket. I crammed it into my waistcoat pocket, and hurried off to see the race. To my intense astonishment "Mrs. Waller" won. The novel sensation of having backed the winner so excited me that I forgot all about my money, and it was not until a good hour afterwards that I recollected my bet.

Then I started off to search for the man under the white umbrella. I went to where I thought I had left him, but no white umbrella could I find.

Consoling myself with the reflection that my loss served me right for having been fool enough to trust an outside "bookie," I turned on my heel and began to make my way back to my seat. Suddenly a voice hailed me:

"Here you are, sir. It's Jack Burridge you want. Over here, sir."

I looked round, and there was Jack Burridge at my elbow.

"I saw you looking about, sir," he said, "but I could not make you hear. You was looking the wrong side of the tent."

It was pleasant to find that his honest face had not belied him.

"It is very good of you," I said; "I had given up all hopes of seeing you. Or," I added with a smile, "my seven pounds."

"Seven pun' ten," he corrected me; "you're forgetting your own thin 'un."

He handed me the money and went back to his stand.

On my way into the town I came across him again. A small crowd was collected, thoughtfully watching a tramp knocking about a miserable-looking woman.

Jack, pushing to the front, took in the scene and took off his coat in the same instant.

"Now then, my fine old English gentleman," he sang out, "come and have a try at me for a change."

The tramp was a burly ruffian, and I have seen better boxers than Jack. He got himself a black eye, and a nasty cut over the lip, before he hardly knew where he was. But in spite of that--and a good deal more--he stuck to his man and finished him.

At the end, as he helped his adversary up, I heard him say to the fellow in a kindly whisper:--

"You're too good a sort, you know, to whollop a woman. Why, you very near give me a licking. You must have forgot yourself, matey."

The fellow interested me. I waited and walked on with him. He told me about his home in London, at Mile End, about his old father and mother, his little brothers and sisters and what he was saving up to do for them. Kindliness oozed from every pore in his skin.

Many that we met knew him, and all, when they saw his round, red face, smiled unconsciously. At the corner of the High Street a pale-faced little drudge of a girl passed us, saying as she slipped by "Good-evening, Mr. Burridge."

He made a dart and caught her by the shoulder.

"And how is father?" he asked.

"Oh, if you please, Mr. Burridge, he is out again. All the mills is closed," answered the child.

"And mother?"

"She don't get no better, sir."

"And who's keeping you all?"

"Oh, if you please, sir, Jimmy's earning something now," replied the mite.

He took a couple of sovereigns from his waistcoat pocket, and closed the child's hand upon them.

"That's all right, my lass, that's all right," he said, stopping her stammering thanks. "You write to me if things don't get better. You know where to find Jack Burridge."

Strolling about the streets in the evening, I happened to pass the inn where he was staying. The parlour window was open, and out into the misty night his deep, cheery voice, trolling forth an old-fashioned drinking song, came rolling like a wind, cleansing the corners of one's heart with its breezy humanness. He was sitting at the head of the table surrounded by a crowd of jovial cronies. I lingered for a while watching the scene. It made the world appear a less sombre dwelling-place than I had sometimes pictured it.

I determined, on my return to London, to look him up, and accordingly one evening started to find the little by-street off the Mile End Road in which he lived. As I turned the corner he drove up in his dog-cart; it was a smart turn-out. On the seat beside him sat a neat, withered little old woman, whom he introduced to me as his mother.

"I tell 'im it's a fine gell as 'e oughter 'ave up 'ere aside 'im," said the old lady, preparing to dismount, "an old woman like me takes all the paint off the show."

"Get along with yer," he replied laughingly, jumping down and handing the reins to the lad who had been waiting, "you could give some of the young uns points yet, mother. I allus promised the old lady as she should ride behind her own 'oss one day," he continued, turning to me, "didn't I, mother?"

"Ay, ay," replied the old soul, as she hobbled nimbly up the steps, "ye're a good son, Jack, ye're a good son."

He led the way into the parlour. As he entered every face lightened up with pleasure, a harmony of joyous welcome greeted him. The old hard world had been shut out with the slam of the front door. I seemed to have wandered into Dickensland. The red-faced man with the small twinkling eyes and the lungs of leather loomed before me, a large, fat household fairy. From his capacious pockets came forth tobacco for the old father; a huge bunch of hot-house grapes for a neighbour's sickly child, who was stopping with them; a book of Henty's--beloved of boys-- for a noisy youngster who called him "uncle"; a bottle of port wine for a wan, elderly woman with a swollen face--his widowed sister-in-law, as I subsequently learned; sweets enough for the baby (whose baby I don't know) to make it sick for a week; and a roll of music for his youngest sister.

"We're a-going to make a lady of her," he said, drawing the child's shy face against his gaudy waistcoat, and running his coarse hand through her pretty curls; "and she shall marry a jockey when she grows up."

After supper he brewed some excellent whisky punch, and insisted upon the old lady joining us, which she eventually did with much coughing and protestation; but I noticed that she finished the tumblerful. For the children he concocted a marvellous mixture, which he called an "eye-composer," the chief ingredients being hot lemonade, ginger wine, sugar, oranges, and raspberry vinegar. It had the desired effect.

I stayed till late, listening to his inexhaustible fund of stories.

Over most of them he laughed with us himself--a great gusty laugh that made the cheap glass ornaments upon the mantelpiece to tremble; but now and then a recollection came to him that spread a sudden gravity across his jovial face, bringing a curious quaver into his deep voice.

Their tongues a little loosened by the punch, the old folks would have sung his praises to the verge of tediousness had he not almost sternly interrupted them.

"Shut up, mother," he cried at last, quite gruffly, "what I does I does to please myself. I likes to see people comfortable about me. If they wasn't, it's me as would be more upset than them."

I did not see him again for nearly two years. Then one October evening, strolling about the East End, I met him coming out of a little Chapel in the Burdett Road. He was so changed that I should not have known him had not I overheard a woman as she passed him say, "Good-evening, Mr. Burridge."

A pair of bushy side-whiskers had given to his red face an aggressively respectable appearance. He was dressed in an ill-fitting suit of black, and carried an umbrella in one hand and a book in the other.

In some mysterious way he managed to look both thinner and shorter than my recollection of him. Altogether, he suggested to me the idea that he himself, the real man, had by some means or other been extracted, leaving only his shrunken husk behind. The genial juices of humanity had been squeezed out of him.

"Not Jack Burridge!" I exclaimed, confronting him in astonishment.

His little eyes wandered shiftily up and down the street. "No, sir," he replied (his tones had lost their windy boisterousness, a hard, metallic voice spoke to me), "not the one as you used to know, praise be the Lord."

"And have you given up the old business?" I asked.

"Yes, sir," he replied, "that's all over; I've been a vile sinner in my time, God forgive me for it. But, thank Heaven, I have repented in time."

"Come and have a drink," I said, slipping my arm through his, "and tell me all about it."

He disengaged himself from me, firmly but gently. "You mean well, sir," he said, "but I have given up the drink."

Evidently he would have been rid of me, but a literary man, scenting material for his stockpot, is not easily shaken off. I asked after the old folks, and if they were still stopping with him.

"Yes," he said, "for the present. Of course, a man can't be expected to keep people for ever; so many mouths to fill is hard work these times, and everybody sponges on a man just because he's good-natured."

"And how are you getting on?" I asked.

"Tolerably well, thank you, sir. The Lord provides for His servants," he replied with a smug smile. "I have got a little shop now in the Commercial Road."

"Whereabouts?" I persisted. "I would like to call and see you."

He gave me the address reluctantly, and said he would esteem it a great pleasure if I would honour him by a visit, which was a palpable lie.

The following afternoon I went. I found the place to be a pawnbroker's shop, and from all appearances he must have been doing a very brisk business. He was out himself attending a temperance committee, but his old father was behind the counter, and asked me inside. Though it was a chilly day there was no fire in the parlour, and the two old folks sat one each side of the empty hearth, silent and sad. They seemed little more pleased to see me than their son, but after a while Mrs. Burridge's natural garrulity asserted itself, and we fell into chat.

I asked what had become of his sister-in-law, the lady with the swollen face.

"I couldn't rightly tell you, sir," answered the old lady, "she ain't livin' with us now. You see, sir," she continued, "John's got different notions to what 'e used to 'ave. 'E don't cotten much to them as ain't found grace, and poor Jane never did 'ave much religion!"

"And the little one?" I inquired. "The one with the curls?"

"What, Bessie, sir?" said the old lady. "Oh, she's out at service, sir; John don't think it good for young folks to be idle."

"Your son seems to have changed a good deal, Mrs. Burridge," I remarked.

"Ay, sir," she assented, "you may well say that. It nearly broke my 'art at fust; everythin' so different to what it 'ad been. Not as I'd stand in the boy's light.

If our being a bit uncomfortable like in this world is a-going to do 'im any good in the next me and father ain't the ones to begrudge it, are we, old man?"

The "old man" concurred grumpily.

"Was it a sudden conversion?" I asked. "How did it come about?"

"It was a young woman as started 'im off," explained the old lady. "She come round to our place one day a-collectin' for somethin' or other, and Jack, in 'is free-'anded way, 'e give 'er a five-pun' note. Next week she come agen for somethin' else, and stopped and talked to 'im about 'is soul in the passage. She told 'im as 'e was a-goin' straight to 'ell, and that 'e oughter give up the bookmakin' and settle down to a respec'ble, God-fearin' business. At fust 'e only laughed, but she lammed in tracts at 'im full of the most awful language; and one day she fetched 'im round to one of them revivalist chaps, as fair settled 'im.

"'E ain't never been his old self since then. 'E give up the bettin' and bought this 'ere, though what's the difference blessed if I can see. It makes my 'eart ache, it do, to 'ear my Jack a-beatin' down the poor people--and it ain't like 'im. It went agen 'is grain at fust, I could see; but they told him as 'ow it was folks's own fault that they was poor, and as 'ow it was the will of God, because they was a drinkin', improvident lot.

"Then they made 'im sign the pledge. 'E'd allus been used to 'is glass, Jack 'ad, and I think as knockin' it off 'ave soured 'im a bit, seems as if all the sperit 'ad gone out of 'im--and of course me and father 'ave 'ad to give up our little drop too. Then they told 'im as 'e must give up smokin'- that was another way of goin' straight to 'ell and that ain't made 'im any the more cheerful like, and father misses 'is little bit--don't ye, father?"

"Ay," answered the old fellow savagely; "can't say I thinks much of these 'ere folks as is going to heaven; blowed if I don't think they'll be a chirpier lot in t'other place."

An angry discussion in the shop interrupted us. Jack had returned, and was threatening an excited woman with the police. It seemed she had miscalculated the date, and had come a day too late with her interest.

Having got rid of her, he came into the parlour with the watch in his hand.

"It's providential she was late," he said, looking at it; "it's worth ten times what I lent on it."

He packed his father back into the shop, and his mother down into the kitchen to get his tea, and for a while we sat together talking.

I found his conversation a strange mixture of self-laudation, showing through a flimsy veil of self-disparagement, and of satisfaction at the conviction that he was "saved," combined with equally evident satisfaction that most other people weren't somewhat trying, however; and, remembering an appointment, rose to go.

He made no effort to stay me, but I could see that he was bursting to tell me something. At last, taking a religious paper from his pocket, and pointing to a column, he blurted out:

"You don't take any interest in the Lord's vineyard, I suppose, sir?"

I glanced at the part of the paper indicated. It announced a new mission to the Chinese, and heading the subscription list stood the name, "Mr. John Burridge, one hundred guineas."

"You subscribe largely, Mr. Burridge," I said, handing him back the paper.

He rubbed his big hands together. "The Lord will repay a hundredfold," he answered.

"In which case it's just as well to have a note of the advance down in black and white, eh?" I added.

His little eyes looked sharply at me; but he made no reply, and, shaking hands, I left him.

The Philosopher's Joke

Myself, I do not believe this story. Six persons are persuaded of its truth; and the hope of these six is to convince themselves it was an hallucination. Their difficulty is there are six of them. Each one alone perceives clearly that it never could have been. Unfortunately, they are close friends, and cannot get away from one another; and when they meet and look into each other's eyes the thing takes shape again.

The one who told it to me, and who immediately wished he had not, was Armitage. He told it to me one night when he and I were the only occupants of the Club smoking-room. His telling me as he explained afterwards was an impulse of the moment.

Sense of the thing had been pressing upon him all that day with unusual persistence; and the idea had occurred to him, on my entering the room, that the flippant scepticism with which an essentially commonplace mind like my own, he used the words in no offensive sense, would be sure to regard the affair might help to direct his own attention to its more absurd aspect. I am inclined to think it did. He thanked me for dismissing his entire narrative as the delusion of a disordered brain, and begged me not to mention the matter to another living soul. I promised; and I may as well here observe that I do not call this mentioning the matter. Armitage is not the man's real name; it does not even begin with an A. You might read this story and dine next to him the same evening: you would know nothing.

Also, of course, I did not consider myself debarred from speaking about it, discreetly, to Mrs. Armitage, a charming woman. She burst into tears at the first mention of the thing. It took me all I knew to tranquillize her. She said that when she did not think about the thing she could be happy. She and Armitage never spoke of it to one another; and left to themselves her opinion was that eventually they might put remembrance behind them. She wished they were not quite so friendly with the Everetts. Mr. and Mrs. Everett had both dreamt precisely the same dream; that is, assuming it was a dream. Mr. Everett was not the sort of person that a clergyman ought, perhaps, to know; but as Armitage would always argue: for a teacher of Christianity to withdraw his friendship from a man because that man was somewhat of a sinner would be inconsistent. Rather should he remain his friend and seek to influence him. They dined with the Everetts regularly on Tuesdays, and sitting opposite the Everetts, it seemed impossible to accept as a fact that all four of them at the same time and in the same manner had fallen victims to the same illusion. I think I succeeded in leaving her more hopeful. She acknowledged that the story, looked at from the point of common sense, did sound ridiculous; and threatened me that if I ever breathed a word of it to anyone, she never would speak to me again. She is a charming woman, as I have already mentioned.

By a curious coincidence I happened at the time to be one of Everett's directors on a Company he had just promoted for taking over and developing the Red Sea Coasting trade. I lunched with him the following Sunday. He is an interesting talker, and curiosity to discover how so shrewd a man would account for his connection with so insane, so impossible a fancy, prompted me to hint my knowledge of the story. The manner both of him and of his wife changed suddenly. They wanted to know who it was had told me. I refused the information, because it was evident they would have been angry with him. Everett's theory was that one of them had dreamt it, probably Camelford, and by hypnotic suggestion had conveyed to the rest of them the impression that they had dreamt it also.

He added that but for one slight incident he should have ridiculed from the very beginning the argument that it could have been anything else than a dream. But what that incident was he would not tell me. His object, as he explained, was not to dwell upon the business, but to try and forget it. Speaking as a friend, he advised me, likewise, not to cackle about the matter any more than I could help, lest trouble should arise with regard to my director's fees. His way of putting things is occasionally blunt.

It was at the Everetts', later on, that I met Mrs. Camelford, one of the handsomest women I have ever set eyes upon. It was foolish of me, but my memory for names is weak. I forgot that Mr. and Mrs. Camelford were the other two concerned, and mentioned the story as a curious tale I had read years ago in an old Miscellany. I had reckoned on it to lead me into a discussion with her on platonic friendship. She jumped up from her chair and gave me a look. I remembered then, and could have bitten out my tongue. It took me a long while to make my peace, but she came round in the end, consenting to attribute my blunder to mere stupidity. She was quite convinced herself, she told me, that the thing was pure imagination. It was only when in company with the others that any doubt as to this crossed her mind. Her own idea was that, if everybody would agree never to mention the matter again, it would end in their forgetting it. She supposed it was her husband who had been my informant: he was just that sort of ass. She did not say it unkindly. She said when she was first married, ten years ago, few people had a more irritating effect upon her than had Camelford; but that since she had seen more of other men she had come to respect him. I like to hear a woman speak well of her husband. It is a departure which, in my opinion, should be more encouraged than it is. I assured her Camelford was not the culprit; and on the understanding that I might come to see her, not too often, on her Thursdays, I agreed with her that the best thing I could do would be to dismiss the subject from my mind and occupy myself instead with questions that concerned myself.

I had never talked much with Camelford before that time, though I had often seen him at the Club. He is a strange man, of whom many stories are told. He writes journalism for a living, and poetry, which he publishes at his own expense, apparently for recreation. It occurred to me that his theory would at all events be interesting; but at first he would not talk at all, pretending to ignore the whole affair, as idle nonsense. I had almost despaired of drawing him out, when one evening, of his own accord, he asked me if I thought Mrs. Armitage, with whom he knew I was on terms of friendship, still attached importance to the thing. On my expressing the opinion that Mrs. Armitage was the most troubled of the group, he was irritated; and urged me to leave the rest of them alone and devote whatever sense I might possess to persuading her in particular that the entire thing was and could be nothing but pure myth.

He confessed frankly that to him it was still a mystery. He could easily regard it as chimera, but for one slight incident. He would not for a long while say what that was, but there is such a thing as perseverance, and in the end I dragged it out of him. This is what he told me.

"We happened by chance to find ourselves alone in the conservatory, that night of the ball we six. Most of the crowd had already left. The last 'extra' was being played: the music came to us faintly. Stooping to pick up Jessica's fan, which she had let fall to the ground, something shining on the tesselated pavement underneath a group of palms suddenly caught my eye. We had not said a word to one another; indeed, it was the first evening we had any of us met one another that is, unless the thing was not a dream. I picked it up. The others gathered round me, and when we looked into one another's eyes we understood: it was a broken wine-cup, a curious goblet of Bavarian glass. It was the goblet out of which we had all dreamt that we had drunk."

I have put the story together as it seems to me it must have happened. The incidents, at all events, are facts. Things have since occurred to those concerned affording me hope that they will never read it. I should not have troubled to tell it at all, but that it has a moral.

Six persons sat round the great oak table in the wainscoted Speise Saal of that cosy hostelry, the Kneiper Hof at Konigsberg. It was late into the night. Under ordinary circumstances they would have been in bed, but having arrived by the last train from Dantzic, and having supped on German fare, it had seemed to them discreeter to remain awhile in talk. The house was strangely silent. The rotund landlord, leaving their candles ranged upon the sideboard, had wished them "Gute Nacht" an hour before. The spirit of the ancient house enfolded them within its wings.

Here in this very chamber, if rumour is to be believed, Emmanuel Kant himself had sat discoursing many a time and oft. The walls, behind which for more than forty years the little peak-faced man had thought and worked, rose silvered by the moonlight just across the narrow way; the three high windows of the Speise Saal give out upon the old Cathedral tower beneath which now he rests. Philosophy, curious concerning human phenomena, eager for experience, unhampered by the limitation Convention would impose upon all speculation, was in the smoky air.

"Not into future events," remarked the Rev. Nathaniel Armitage, "it is better they should be hidden from us. But into the future of ourselves; our temperament, our character, I think we ought to be allowed to see.

At twenty we are one individual; at forty, another person entirely, with other views, with other interests, a different outlook upon life, attracted by quite other attributes, repelled by the very qualities that once attracted us. It is extremely awkward, for all of us."

"I am glad to hear somebody else say that," observed Mrs. Everett, in her gentle, sympathetic voice. "I have thought it all myself so often.

Sometimes I have blamed myself, yet how can one help it: the things that appeared of importance to us, they become indifferent; new voices call to us; the idols we once worshipped, we see their feet of clay."

"If under the head of idols you include me," laughed the jovial Mr. Everett, "don't hesitate to say so." He was a large red-faced gentleman, with small twinkling eyes, and a mouth both strong and sensuous. "I didn't make my feet myself. I never asked anybody to take me for a stained-glass saint. It is not I who have changed."

"I know, dear, it is I," his thin wife answered with a meek smile. "I was beautiful, there was no doubt about it, when you married me."

"You were, my dear," agreed her husband: "As a girl few could hold a candle to you."

"It was the only thing about me that you valued, my beauty," continued his wife; "and it went so quickly. I feel sometimes as if I had swindled you."

"But there is a beauty of the mind, of the soul," remarked the Rev. Nathaniel Armitage, "that to some men is more attractive than mere physical perfection."

The soft eyes of the faded lady shone for a moment with the light of pleasure. "I am afraid Dick is not of that number," she sighed.

"Well, as I said just now about my feet," answered her husband genially, "I didn't make myself. I always have been a slave to beauty and always shall be. There would be no sense in pretending among chums that you haven't lost your looks, old girl." He laid his fine hand with kindly intent upon her bony shoulder. "But there is no call for you to fret yourself as if you had done it on purpose. No one but a lover imagines a woman growing more beautiful as she grows older."

"Some women would seem to," answered his wife.

Involuntarily she glanced to where Mrs. Camelford sat with elbows resting on the table; and involuntarily also the small twinkling eyes of her husband followed in the same direction.

There is a type that reaches its prime in middle age. Mrs. Camelford, nee Jessica Dearwood, at twenty had been an uncanny-looking creature, the only thing about her appealing to general masculine taste having been her magnificent eyes, and even these had frightened more than they had allured. At forty, Mrs. Camelford might have posed for the entire Juno.

"Yes, he's a cunning old joker is Time," murmured Mr. Everett, almost inaudibly.

"What ought to have happened," said Mrs. Armitage, while with deft fingers rolling herself a cigarette, "was for you and Nellie to have married."

Mrs. Everett's pale face flushed scarlet.

"My dear," exclaimed the shocked Nathaniel Armitage, flushing likewise.

"Oh, why may one not sometimes speak the truth?" answered his wife petulantly. "You and I are utterly unsuited to one another--everybody sees it. At nineteen it seemed to me beautiful, holy, the idea of being a clergyman's wife, fighting by his side against evil. Besides, you have changed since then. You were human, my dear Nat, in those days, and the best dancer I had ever met. It was your dancing was your chief attraction for me as likely as not, if I had only known myself. At nineteen how can one know oneself?"

"We loved each other," the Rev. Armitage reminded her.

"I know we did, passionately then; but we don't now." She laughed a little bitterly. "Poor Nat! I am only another trial added to your long list. Your beliefs, your ideals are meaningless to me, mere narrow-minded dogmas, stifling thought. Nellie was the wife Nature had intended for you, so soon as she had lost her beauty and with it all her worldly ideas. Fate was maturing her for you, if only we had known. As for me, I ought to have been the wife of an artist, of a poet." Unconsciously a glance from her ever restless eyes flashed across the table to where Horatio Camelford sat, puffing clouds of smoke into the air from a huge black meerschaum pipe. "Bohemia is my country. Its poverty, its struggle would have been a joy to me. Breathing its free air, life would have been worth living."

Horatio Camelford leant back with eyes fixed on the oaken ceiling. "It is a mistake," said Horatio Camelford, "for the artist ever to marry."

The handsome Mrs. Camelford laughed good-naturedly. "The artist," remarked Mrs. Camelford, "from what I have seen of him would never know the inside of his shirt from the outside if his wife was not there to take it out of the drawer and put it over his head."

"His wearing it inside out would not make much difference to the world," argued her husband. "The sacrifice of his art to the necessity of keeping his wife and family does."

"Well, you at all events do not appear to have sacrificed much, my boy," came the breezy voice of Dick Everett. "Why, all the world is ringing with your name."

"When I am forty-one, with all the best years of my life behind me," answered the Poet. "Speaking as a man, I have nothing to regret. No one could have had a better wife; my children are charming. I have lived the peaceful existence of the successful citizen. Had I been true to my trust I should have gone out into the wilderness, the only possible home of the teacher, the prophet. The artist is the bridegroom of Art. Marriage for him is an immorality. Had I my time again I should remain a bachelor."

"Time brings its revenges, you see," laughed Mrs. Camelford. "At twenty that fellow threatened to commit suicide if I would not marry him, and cordially disliking him I consented. Now twenty years later, when I am just getting used to him, he calmly turns round and says he would have been better without me."

"I heard something about it at the time," said Mrs. Armitage. "You were very much in love with somebody else, were you not?"

"Is not the conversation assuming a rather dangerous direction?" laughed Mrs. Camelford.

"I was thinking the same thing," agreed Mrs. Everett. "One would imagine some strange influence had seized upon us, forcing us to speak our thoughts aloud."

"I am afraid I was the original culprit," admitted the Reverend Nathaniel. "This room is becoming quite oppressive. Had we not better go to bed?"

The ancient lamp suspended from its smoke-grimed beam uttered a faint, gurgling sob, and spluttered out. The shadow of the old Cathedral tower crept in and stretched across the room, now illuminated only by occasional beams from the cloud-curtained moon. At the other end of the table sat a peak-faced little gentleman, clean-shaven, in full-bottomed wig.

"Forgive me," said the little gentleman. He spoke in English, with a strong accent. "But it seems to me here is a case where two parties might be of service to one another."

The six fellow-travellers round the table looked at one another, but none spoke. The idea that came to each of them, as they explained to one another later, was that without remembering it they had taken their candles and had gone to bed. This was surely a dream.

"It would greatly assist me," continued the little peak-faced gentleman, "in experiments I am conducting into the phenomena of human tendencies, if you would allow me to put your lives back twenty years."

Still no one of the six replied. It seemed to them that the little old gentleman must have been sitting there among them all the time, unnoticed by them.

"Judging from your talk this evening," continued the peak-faced little gentleman, "you should welcome my offer. You appear to me to be one and all of exceptional intelligence. You perceive the mistakes that you have made: you understand the causes. The future veiled, you could not help yourselves. What I propose to do is to put you back twenty years. You will be boys and girls again, but with this difference: that the knowledge of the future, so far as it relates to yourselves, will remain with you.

"Come," urged the old gentleman, "the thing is quite simple of accomplishment. As - as a certain philosopher has clearly proved: the universe is only the result of our own perceptions. By what may appear to you to be magic, by what in reality will be simply a chemical operation, I remove from your memory the events of the last twenty years, with the exception of what immediately concerns your own personalities. You will retain all knowledge of the changes, physical and mental, that will be in store for you; all else will pass from your perception."

The little old gentleman took a small phial from his waistcoat pocket, and, filling one of the massive wine-glasses from a decanter, measured into it some half-a-dozen drops. Then he placed the glass in the centre of the table.

"Youth is a good time to go back to," said the peak-faced little gentleman, with a smile. "Twenty years ago, it was the night of the Hunt Ball. You remember it?"

It was Everett who drank first. He drank it with his little twinkling eyes fixed hungrily on the proud handsome face of Mrs. Camelford; and then handed the glass to his wife.

It was she perhaps who drank from it most eagerly. Her life with Everett, from the day when she had risen from a bed of sickness stripped of all her beauty, had been one bitter wrong. She drank with the wild hope that the thing might possibly be not a dream; and thrilled to the touch of the man she loved, as reaching across the table he took the glass from her hand. Mrs. Armitage was the fourth to drink. She took the cup from her husband, drank with a quiet smile, and passed it on to Camelford. And Camelford drank, looking at nobody, and replaced the glass upon the table.

"Come," said the little old gentleman to Mrs. Camelford, "you are the only one left. The whole thing will be incomplete without you."

"I have no wish to drink," said Mrs. Camelford, and her eyes sought those of her husband, but he would not look at her.

"Come," again urged the Figure. And then Camelford looked at her and laughed drily.

"You had better drink," he said. "It's only a dream."

"If you wish it," she answered. And it was from his hands she took the glass.

It is from the narrative as Armitage told it to me that night in the Club smoking-room that I am taking most of my material. It seemed to him that all things began slowly to rise upward, leaving him stationary, but with a great pain as though the inside of him were being torn away, the same sensation greatly exaggerated, so he likened it, as descending in a lift. But around him all the time was silence and darkness unrelieved. After a period that might have been minutes, that might have been years, a faint light crept towards him. It grew stronger, and into the air which now fanned his cheek there stole the sound of far-off music. The light and the music both increased, and one by one his senses came back to him. He was seated on a low cushioned bench beneath a group of palms. A young girl was sitting beside him, but her face was turned away from him.

"I did not catch your name," he was saying. "Would you mind telling it to me?"

She turned her face towards him. It was the most spiritually beautiful face he had ever seen. "I am in the same predicament," she laughed. "You had better write yours on my programme, and I will write mine on yours."

So they wrote upon each other's programme and exchanged again. The name she had written was Alice Blatchley.

He had never seen her before, that he could remember. Yet at the back of his mind there dwelt the haunting knowledge of her. Somewhere long ago they had met, talked together. Slowly, as one recalls a dream, it came back to him. In some other life, vague, shadowy, he had married this woman. For the first few years they had loved each other; then the gulf had opened between them, widened. Stern, strong voices had called to him to lay aside his selfish dreams, his boyish ambitions, to take upon his shoulders the yoke of a great duty. When more than ever he had demanded sympathy and help, this woman had fallen away from him. His ideals but irritated her. Only at the cost of daily bitterness had he been able to resist her endeavours to draw him from his path. A face that of a woman with soft eyes, full of helpfulness, shone through the mist of his dream, the face of a woman who would one day come to him out of the Future with outstretched hands that he would yearn to clasp.

"Shall we not dance?" said the voice beside him. "I really won't sit out a waltz."

They hurried into the ball-room. With his arm about her form, her wondrous eyes shyly, at rare moments, seeking his, then vanishing again behind their drooping lashes, the brain, the mind, the very soul of the young man passed out of his own keeping. She complimented him in her bewitching manner, a delightful blending of condescension and timidity.

"You dance extremely well," she told him. "You may ask me for another, later on."

The words flashed out from that dim haunting future. "Your dancing was your chief attraction for me, as likely as not, had I but known?"

All that evening and for many months to come the Present and the Future fought within him. And the experience of Nathaniel Armitage, divinity student, was the experience likewise of Alice Blatchley, who had fallen in love with him at first sight, having found him the divinest dancer she had ever whirled with to the sensuous music of the waltz; of Horatio Camelford, journalist and minor poet, whose journalism earned him a bare income, but at whose minor poetry critics smiled; of Jessica Dearwood, with her glorious eyes, and muddy complexion, and her wild hopeless passion for the big, handsome, ruddy-bearded Dick Everett, who, knowing it, only laughed at her in his kindly, lordly way, telling her with frank brutalness that the woman who was not beautiful had missed her vocation in life; of that scheming, conquering young gentleman himself, who at twenty-five had already made his mark in the City, shrewd, clever, cool-headed as a fox, except where a pretty face and shapely hand or ankle were concerned; of Nellie Fanshawe, then in the pride of her ravishing beauty, who loved none but herself, whose clay-made gods were jewels, and fine dresses and rich feasts, the envy of other women and the courtship of all mankind.

That evening of the ball each clung to the hope that this memory of the future was but a dream. They had been introduced to one another; had heard each other's names for the first time with a start of recognition; had avoided one another's eyes; had hastened to plunge into meaningless talk; till that moment when young Camelford, stooping to pick up Jessica's fan, had found that broken fragment of the Rhenish wine-glass. Then it was that conviction refused to be shaken off, that knowledge of the future had to be sadly accepted.

What they had not foreseen was that knowledge of the future in no way affected their emotions of the present. Nathaniel Armitage grew day by day more hopelessly in love with bewitching Alice Blatchley. The thought of her marrying anyone else the long-haired, priggish Camelford in particular sent the blood boiling through his veins; added to which sweet Alice, with her arms about his neck, would confess to him that life without him would be a misery hardly to be endured, that the thought of him as the husband of another woman of Nellie Fanshawe in particular was madness to her. It was right perhaps, knowing what they did, that they should say good-bye to one another. She would bring sorrow into his life. Better far that he should put her away from him, that she should die of a broken heart, as she felt sure she would. How could he, a fond lover, inflict this suffering upon her? He ought of course to marry Nellie Fanshawe, but he could not bear the girl. Would it not be the height of absurdity to marry a girl he strongly disliked because twenty years hence she might be more suitable to him than the woman he now loved and who loved him?

Nor could Nellie Fanshawe bring herself to discuss without laughter the suggestion of marrying on a hundred-and-fifty a year a curate that she positively hated. There would come a time when wealth would be indifferent to her, when her exalted spirit would ask but for the satisfaction of self-sacrifice. But that time had not arrived. The emotions it would bring with it she could not in her present state even imagine. Her whole present being craved for the things of this world, the things that were within her grasp. To ask her to forego them now because later on she would not care for them! it was like telling a schoolboy to avoid the tuck-shop because, when a man, the thought of stick-jaw would be nauseous to him. If her capacity for enjoyment was to be short-lived, all the more reason for grasping joy quickly.

Alice Blatchley, when her lover was not by, gave herself many a headache trying to think the thing out logically. Was it not foolish of her to rush into this marriage with dear Nat? At forty she would wish she had married somebody else. But most women at forty, she judged from conversation round about her, wished they had married somebody else. If every girl at twenty listened to herself at forty there would be no more marriage. At forty she would be a different person altogether. That other elderly person did not interest her. To ask a young girl to spoil her life purely in the interests of this middle-aged party, it did not seem right. Besides, whom else was she to marry? Camelford would not have her; he did not want her then; he was not going to want her at forty. For practical purposes Camelford was out of the question. She might marry somebody else altogether and fare worse. She might remain a spinster: she hated the mere name of spinster. The inky-fingered woman journalist that, if all went well, she might become: it was not her idea. Was she acting selfishly? Ought she, in his own interests, to refuse to marry dear Nat? Nellie, the little cat, who would suit him at forty, would not have him. If he was going to marry anyone but Nellie he might as well marry her, Alice. A bachelor clergyman! it sounded almost improper. Nor was dear Nat the type. If she threw him over it would be into the arms of some designing minx. What was she to do?

Camelford at forty, under the influence of favourable criticism, would have persuaded himself he was a heaven-sent prophet, his whole life to be beautifully spent in the saving of mankind. At twenty he felt he wanted to live. Weird-looking Jessica, with her magnificent eyes veiling mysteries, was of more importance to him than the rest of the species combined. Knowledge of the future in his ease only spurred desire. The muddy complexion would grow pink and white, the thin limbs round and shapely; the now scornful eyes would one day light with love at his coming. It was what he had once hoped: it was what he now knew. At forty the artist is stronger than the man; at twenty the man is stronger than the artist.

An uncanny creature, so most folks would have described Jessica Dearwood. Few would have imagined her developing into the good-natured, easy-going Mrs. Camelford of middle age. The animal, so strong within her at twenty, at thirty had burnt itself out. At eighteen, madly, blindly in love with red-bearded, deep-voiced Dick Everett she would, had he whistled to her, have flung herself gratefully at his feet, and this in spite of the knowledge forewarning her of the miserable life he would certainly lead her, at all events until her slowly developing beauty should give her the whip hand of him by which time she would have come to despise him. Fortunately, as she told herself, there was no fear of his doing so, the future notwithstanding. Nellie Fanshawe's beauty held him as with chains of steel, and Nellie had no intention of allowing her rich prize to escape her.

Her own lover, it was true, irritated her more than any man she had ever met, but at least he would afford her refuge from the bread of charity. Jessica Dearwood, an orphan, had been brought up by a distant relative. She had not been the child to win affection. Of silent, brooding nature, every thoughtless incivility had been to her an insult, a wrong.

Acceptance of young Camelford seemed her only escape from a life that had become to her a martyrdom. At forty-one he would wish he had remained a bachelor; but at thirty-eight that would not trouble her. She would know herself he was much better off as he was. Meanwhile, she would have come to like him, to respect him. He would be famous, she would be proud of him. Crying into her pillow, she could not help it, for love of handsome Dick, it was still a comfort to reflect that Nellie Fanshawe, as it were, was watching over her, protecting her from herself.

Dick, as he muttered to himself a dozen times a day, ought to marry Jessica. At thirty-eight she would be his ideal. He looked at her as she was at eighteen, and shuddered. Nellie at thirty would be plain and uninteresting. But when did consideration of the future ever cry halt to passion: when did a lover ever pause thinking of the morrow? If her beauty was to quickly pass, was not that one reason the more urging him to possess it while it lasted?

Nellie Fanshawe at forty would be a saint. The prospect did not please her: she hated saints. She would love the tiresome, solemn Nathaniel: of what use was that to her now? He did not desire her; he was in love with Alice, and Alice was in love with him. What would be the sense, even if they all agreed in the three of them making themselves miserable for all their youth that they might be contented in their old age? Let age fend for itself and leave youth to its own instincts. Let elderly saints suffer it was their metier and youth drink the cup of life. It was a pity Dick was the only "catch" available, but he was young and handsome. Other girls had to put up with sixty and the gout.

Another point, a very serious point, had been overlooked. All that had arrived to them in that dim future of the past had happened to them as the results of their making the marriages they had made. To what fate other roads would lead their knowledge could not tell them. Nellie Fanshawe had become at forty a lovely character. Might not the hard life she had led with her husband, a life calling for continual sacrifice, for daily self-control, have helped towards this end? As the wife of a poor curate of high moral principles, would the same result have been secured? The fever that had robbed her of her beauty and turned her thoughts inward had been the result of sitting out on the balcony of the Paris Opera House with an Italian Count on the occasion of a fancy dress ball. As the wife of an East End clergyman the chances are she would have escaped that fever and its purifying effects.

Was there not danger in the position: a supremely beautiful young woman, worldly-minded, hungry for pleasure, condemned to a life of poverty with a man she did not care for? The influence of Alice upon Nathaniel Armitage, during those first years when his character was forming, had been all for good. Could he be sure that, married to Nellie, he might not have deteriorated?

Were Alice Blatchley to marry an artist could she be sure that at forty she would still be in sympathy with artistic ideals? Even as a child had not her desire ever been in the opposite direction to that favoured by her nurse? Did not the reading of Conservative journals invariably incline her towards Radicalism, and the steady stream of Radical talk round her husband's table invariably set her seeking arguments in favour of the feudal system? Might it not have been her husband's growing Puritanism that had driven her to crave for Bohemianism? Suppose that towards middle age, the wife of a wild artist, she suddenly "took religion," as the saying is. Her last state would be worse than the first.

Camelford was of delicate physique. As an absent-minded bachelor with no one to give him his meals, no one to see that his things were aired, could he have lived till forty? Could he be sure that home life had not given more to his art than it had taken from it?

Jessica Dearwood, of a nervous, passionate nature, married to a bad husband, might at forty have posed for one of the Furies. Not until her life had become restful had her good looks shown themselves. Hers was the type of beauty that for its development demands tranquillity.

Dick Everett had no delusions concerning himself. That, had he married Jessica, he could for ten years have remained the faithful husband of a singularly plain wife he knew to be impossible. But Jessica would have been no patient Griselda. The extreme probability was that having married her at twenty for the sake of her beauty at thirty, at twenty-nine at latest she would have divorced him.

Everett was a man of practical ideas. It was he who took the matter in hand. The refreshment contractor admitted that curious goblets of German glass occasionally crept into their stock. One of the waiters, on the understanding that in no case should he be called upon to pay for them, admitted having broken more than one wine-glass on that particular evening: thought it not unlikely he might have attempted to hide the fragments under a convenient palm. The whole thing evidently was a dream. So youth decided at the time, and the three marriages took place within three months of one another.

It was some ten years later that Armitage told me the story that night in the Club smoking-room. Mrs. Everett had just recovered from a severe attack of rheumatic fever, contracted the spring before in Paris. Mrs. Camelford, whom previously I had not met, certainly seemed to me one of the handsomest women I have ever seen. Mrs. Armitage, I knew her when she was Alice Blatchley, I found more charming as a woman than she had been as a girl. What she could have seen in Armitage I never could understand. Camelford made his mark some ten years later: poor fellow, he did not live long to enjoy his fame. Dick Everett has still another six years to work off; but he is well behaved, and there is talk of a petition.

It is a curious story altogether, I admit. As I said at the beginning, I do not myself believe it.

The Minor Poet's Story

"It doesn't suit you at all," I answered.

"You're very disagreeable," said she, "I shan't ever ask your advice again."

"Nobody," I hastened to add, "would look well in it. You, of course, look less awful in it than any other woman would, but it's not your style."

"He means," exclaimed the Minor Poet, "that the thing itself not being pre-eminently beautiful, it does not suit, is not in agreement with you. The contrast between you and anything approaching the ugly or the commonplace, is too glaring to be aught else than displeasing."

"He didn't say it," replied the Woman of the World; "and besides it isn't ugly. It's the very latest fashion."

"Why is it," asked the Philosopher, "that women are such slaves to fashion? They think clothes, they talk clothes, they read clothes, yet they have never understood clothes. The purpose of dress, after the primary object of warmth has been secured, is to adorn, to beautify the particular wearer. Yet not one woman in a thousand stops to consider what colours will go best with her complexion, what cut will best hide the defects or display the advantages of her figure. If it be the fashion, she must wear it. And so we have pale-faced girls looking ghastly in shades suitable to dairy-maids, and dots waddling about in costumes fit and proper to six-footers. It is as if crows insisted on wearing cockatoo's feathers on their heads, and rabbits ran about with peacocks' tails fastened behind them."

"And are not you men every bit as foolish?" retorted the Girton Girl. "Sack coats come into fashion, and dumpy little men trot up and down in them, looking like butter-tubs on legs. You go about in July melting under frock-coats and chimney-pot hats, and because it is the stylish thing to do, you all play tennis in still shirts and stand-up collars, which is idiotic. If fashion decreed that you should play cricket in a pair of top-boots and a diver's helmet, you would play cricket in a pair of top-boots and a diver's helmet, and dub every sensible fellow who didn't a cad. It's worse in you than in us; men are supposed to think for themselves, and to be capable of it, the womanly woman isn't."

"Big women and little men look well in nothing," said the Woman of the World. "Poor Emily was five foot ten and a half, and never looked an inch under seven foot, whatever she wore. Empires came into fashion, and the poor child looked like the giant's baby in a pantomime. We thought the Greek might help her, but it only suggested a Crystal Palace statue tied up in a sheet, and tied up badly; and when puff-sleeves and shoulder-capes were in and Teddy stood up behind her at a water-party and sang 'Under the spreading chestnut-tree,' she took it as a personal insult and boxed his ears. Few men liked to be seen with her, and I'm sure George proposed to her partly with the idea of saving himself the expense of a step-ladder, she reaches down his boots for him from the top shelf."

"I," said the Minor Poet, "take up the position of not wanting to waste my brain upon the subject. Tell me what to wear, and I will wear it, and there is an end of the matter. If Society says, 'Wear blue shirts and white collars,' I wear blue shirts and white collars. If she says, 'The time has now come when hats should be broad-brimmed,' I take unto myself a broad-brimmed hat. The question does not interest me sufficiently for me to argue it. It is your fop who refuses to follow fashion. He wishes to attract attention to himself by being peculiar. A novelist whose books pass unnoticed, gains distinction by designing his own necktie; and many an artist, following the line of least resistance, learns to let his hair grow instead of learning to paint."

"The fact is," remarked the Philosopher, "we are the mere creatures of fashion. Fashion dictates to us our religion, our morality, our affections, our thoughts. In one age successful cattle-lifting is a virtue, a few hundred years later company-promoting takes its place as a respectable and legitimate business. In England and America Christianity is fashionable, in Turkey, Mohammedanism, and 'the crimes of Clapham are chaste in Martaban.' In Japan a woman dresses down to the knees, but would be considered immodest if she displayed bare arms. In Europe it is legs that no pure-minded woman is supposed to possess. In China we worship our mother-in-law and despise our wife; in England we treat our wife with respect, and regard our mother-in-law as the bulwark of comic journalism.

The stone age, the iron age, the age of faith, the age of infidelism, the philosophic age, what are they but the passing fashions of the world? It is fashion, fashion, fashion wherever we turn. Fashion waits beside our cradle to lead us by the hand through life. Now literature is sentimental, now hopefully humorous, now psychological, now new-womanly. Yesterday's pictures are the laughing-stock of the up-to-date artist of to-day, and to-day's art will be sneered at to-morrow. Now it is fashionable to be democratic, to pretend that no virtue or wisdom can exist outside corduroy, and to abuse the middle classes. One season we go slumming, and the next we are all socialists. We think we are thinking; we are simply dressing ourselves up in words we do not understand for the gods to laugh at us."

"Don't be pessimistic," retorted the Minor Poet, "pessimism is going out. You call such changes fashions, I call them the footprints of progress. Each phase of thought is an advance upon the former, bringing the footsteps of the many nearer to the landmarks left by the mighty climbers of the past upon the mountain paths of truth. The crowd that was satisfied with The Derby Day now appreciates Millet. The public that were content to wag their heads to The Bohemian Girl have made Wagner popular."

"And the play lovers, who stood for hours to listen to Shakespeare," interrupted the Philosopher, "now crowd to music-halls."

"The track sometimes descends for a little way, but it will wind upwards again," returned the Poet. "The music-hall itself is improving; I consider it the duty of every intellectual man to visit such places. The mere influence of his presence helps to elevate the tone of the performance. I often go myself!"

"I was looking," said the Woman of the World, "at some old illustrated papers of thirty years ago, showing the men dressed in those very absurd trousers, so extremely roomy about the waist, and so extremely tight about the ankles. I recollect poor papa in them; I always used to long to fill them out by pouring in sawdust at the top."

"You mean the peg-top period," I said. "I remember them distinctly myself, but it cannot be more than three-and-twenty years ago at the outside."

"That is very nice of you," replied the Woman of the World, "and shows more tact than I should have given you credit for. It could, as you say, have been only twenty-three years ago. I know I was a very little girl at the time. I think there must be some subtle connection between clothes and thought.

I cannot imagine men in those trousers and Dundreary whiskers talking as you fellows are talking now, any more than I could conceive of a woman in a crinoline and a poke bonnet smoking a cigarette. I think it must be so, because dear mother used to be the most easy-going woman in the world in her ordinary clothes, and would let papa smoke all over the house. But about once every three weeks she would put on a hideous old-fashioned black silk dress, that looked as if Queen Elizabeth must have slept in it during one of those seasons when she used to go about sleeping anywhere, and then we all had to sit up. 'Look out, ma's got her black silk dress on,' came to be a regular formula. We could always make papa take us out for a walk or a drive by whispering it to him."

"I can never bear to look at those pictures of by-gone fashions," said the Old Maid, "I see the by-gone people in them, and it makes me feel as though the faces that we love are only passing fashions with the rest. We wear them for a little while upon our hearts, and think so much of them, and then there comes a time when we lay them by, and forget them, and newer faces take their place, and we are satisfied. It seems so sad."

"I wrote a story some years ago," remarked the Minor Poet, "about a young Swiss guide, who was betrothed to a laughing little French peasant girl."

"Named Suzette," interrupted the Girton Girl. "I know her. Go on."

"Named Jeanne," corrected the Poet, "the majority of laughing French girls, in fiction, are named Suzette, I am well aware. But this girl's mother's family was English. She was christened Jeanne after an aunt Jane, who lived in Birmingham, and from whom she had expectations."

"I beg your pardon," apologised the Girton Girl, "I was not aware of that fact. What happened to her?"

"One morning, a few days before the date fixed for the wedding," said the Minor Poet, "she started off to pay a visit to a relative living in the village, the other side of the mountain. It was a dangerous track, climbing half-way up the mountain before it descended again, and skirting more than one treacherous slope, but the girl was mountain born and bred, sure-footed as a goat, and no one dreamed of harm."

"She went over, of course," said the Philosopher, "those sure-footed girls always do."

"What happened," replied the Minor Poet, "was never known. The girl was never seen again."

"And what became of her lover?" asked the Girton Girl. "Was he, when next year's snow melted, and the young men of the village went forth to gather Edelweiss, wherewith to deck their sweethearts, found by them dead, beside her, at the bottom of the crevasse?"

"No," said the Poet; "you do not know this story, you had better let me tell it. Her lover returned the morning before the wedding day, to be met with the news. He gave way to no sign of grief, he repelled all consolation. Taking his rope and axe he went up into the mountain by himself. All through the winter he haunted the track by which she must have travelled, indifferent to the danger that he ran, impervious apparently to cold, or hunger, or fatigue, undeterred by storm, or mist, or avalanche. At the beginning of the spring he returned to the village, purchased building utensils, and day after day carried them back with him up into the mountain. He hired no labour, he rejected the proffered assistance of his brother guides. Choosing an almost inaccessible spot, at the edge of the great glacier, far from all paths, he built himself a hut, with his own hands; and there for eighteen years he lived alone.

"In the 'season' he earned good fees, being known far and wide as one of the bravest and hardiest of all the guides, but few of his clients liked him, for he was a silent, gloomy man, speaking little, and with never a laugh or jest on the journey. Each fall, having provisioned himself, he would retire to his solitary hut, and bar the door, and no human soul would set eyes on him again until the snows melted.

"One year, however, as the spring days wore on, and he did not appear among the guides, as was his wont, the elder men, who remembered his story and pitied him, grew uneasy; and, after much deliberation, it was determined that a party of them should force their way up to his eyrie. They cut their path across the ice where no foot among them had trodden before, and finding at length the lonely snow-encompassed hut, knocked loudly with their axe-staves on the door; but only the whirling echoes from the glacier's thousand walls replied, so the foremost put his strong shoulder to the worn timber and the door flew open with a crash.

"They found him dead, as they had more than half expected, lying stiff and frozen on the rough couch at the farther end of the hut; and, beside him, looking down upon him with a placid face, as a mother might watch beside her sleeping child, stood Jeanne. She wore the flowers pinned to her dress that she had gathered when their eyes had last seen her. The girl's face that had laughed back to their good-bye in the village, nineteen years ago.

"A strange steely light clung round her, half illuminating, half obscuring her, and the men drew back in fear, thinking they saw a vision, till one, bolder than the rest, stretched out his hand and touched the ice that formed her coffin.

"For eighteen years the man had lived there with this face that he had loved. A faint flush still lingered on the fair cheeks, the laughing lips were still red. Only at one spot, above her temple, the wavy hair lay matted underneath a clot of blood."

The Minor Poet ceased.

"What a very unpleasant way of preserving one's love!" said the Girton Girl.

"When did the story appear?" I asked. "I don't remember reading it."

"I never published it," explained the Minor Poet. "Within the same week two friends of mine, one of whom had just returned from Norway and the other from Switzerland, confided to me their intention of writing stories about girls who had fallen into glaciers, and who had been found by their friends long afterwards, looking as good as new; and a few days later I chanced upon a book, the heroine of which had been dug out of a glacier alive three hundred years after she had fallen in. There seemed to be a run on ice maidens, and I decided not to add to their number."

"It is curious," said the Philosopher, "how there seems to be a fashion even in thought. An idea has often occurred to me that has seemed to me quite new, and taking up a newspaper I have found that some man in Russia or San Francisco has just been saying the very same thing in almost the very same words. We say a thing is 'in the air'; it is more true than we are aware of. Thought does not grow in us. It is a thing apart, we simply gather it. All truths, all discoveries, all inventions, they have not come to us from any one man. The time grows ripe for them, and from this corner of the earth and from that, hands, guided by some instinct, grope for and grasp them. Buddha and Christ seize hold of the morality needful to civilisation, and promulgate it, unknown to one another, the one on the shores of the Ganges, the other by the Jordan. A dozen forgotten explorers, feeling America, prepared the way for Columbus to discover it. A deluge of blood is required to sweep away old follies, and Rousseau and Voltaire, and a myriad others are set to work to fashion the storm clouds. The steam-engine, the spinning loom is 'in the air.' A thousand brains are busy with them, a few go further than the rest. It is idle to talk of human thought; there is no such thing. Our minds are fed as our bodies with the food God has provided for us. Thought hangs by the wayside, and we pick it and cook it, and eat it, and cry out what clever 'thinkers' we are!"

"I cannot agree with you," replied the Minor Poet, "if we were simply automata, as your argument would suggest, what was the purpose of creating us?"

"The intelligent portion of mankind has been asking itself that question for many ages," returned the Philosopher.

"I hate people who always think as I do," said the Girton Girl; "there was a girl in our corridor who never would disagree with me. Every opinion I expressed turned out to be her opinion also. It always irritated me."

"That might have been weak-mindedness," said the Old Maid, which sounded ambiguous.

"It is not so unpleasant as having a person always disagreeing with you," said the Woman of the World. "My cousin Susan never would agree with any one. If I came down in red she would say, 'Why don't you try green, dear? every one says you look so well in green'; and when I wore green she would say, 'Why have you given up red dear? I thought you rather fancied yourself in red.' When I told her of my engagement to Tom, she burst into tears and said she couldn't help it. She had always felt that George and I were intended for one another; and when Tom never wrote for two whole months, and behaved disgracefully in, in other ways, and I told her I was engaged to George, she reminded me of every word I had ever said about my affection for Tom, and of how I had ridiculed poor George. Papa used to say, 'If any man ever tells Susan that he loves her, she will argue him out of it, and will never accept him until he has jilted her, and will refuse to marry him every time he asks her to fix the day.'"

"Is she married?" asked the Philosopher.

"Oh, yes," answered the Woman of the World, "and is devoted to her children. She lets them do everything they don't want to."